In the
Forbidden City

In the
Forbidden City

An Anthology of Erotic

Fiction by Italian Women

Edited by Maria Rosa Cutrufelli

Translated by Vincent J. Bertolini

The University of Chicago Press / Chicago and London

MARIA ROSA CUTRUFELLI is the author of volumes of short fiction and novels, including *Canto al deserto: Storia di Tina, soldato di mafia; Il denaro in corpo. Uomini e donne: La domanda di sesso commerciale;* and *Il paese dei figli perduti: Una ragazza in viaggio nella terra del tempo del sogno.*

VINCENT J. BERTOLINI is a William Rainey Harper Fellow and teaches humanities at the University of Chicago. He is a scholar of nineteenth-century American literature and culture and the translator of *Searching for Emma: Gustave Flaubert and Madame Bovary* by Dacia Maraini (University of Chicago Press, 1998).

The University of Chicago Press, Chicago 60637
The University of Chicago Press, Ltd., London
© 2000 by The University of Chicago
All rights reserved. Published 2000
Printed in the United States of America

09 08 07 06 05 04 03 02 01 00   1 2 3 4 5
ISBN: 0-226-13223-4 (cloth)
ISBN: 0-226-13224-2 (paper)

Originally published as *Nella città proibita: Quattordici scrittrici italiane narrano l'erotismo, il desiderio, la seduzione*
© 1997 Marco Tropea Editore s.r.l. Milano

Library of Congress Cataloging-in-Publication Data

Nella città proibita. English
    In the forbidden city: an anthology of erotic fiction by Italian women / edited by Maria Rosa Cutrufelli ; translated by Vincent J. Bertolini.
        p. cm.
    ISBN 0-226-13223-4 (alk. paper) — ISBN 0-226-13224-2 (alk. paper)
    1. Erotic stories, Italian—Women authors—Translations into English. 2. Italian fiction—20th century—Translations into English. I. Cutrufelli, Maria Rosa. II. Bertolini, Vincent J. III. Title

PQ4249.6.E75 N4513 2000
853'.01083538'082—dc21

                                                    00-024265

CONTENTS

TRANSLATOR'S

ACKNOWLEDGMENTS

I would like to gratefully acknowledge Davide Papotti, Rebecca West of the University of Chicago, and Franco Nasi of the Italian Cultural Institute of Chicago for their generous assistance with certain difficulties that arose in the preparation of this translation. And I would also like to thank Maia Rigas of the University of Chicago Press for her attentive reading and thoughtful editing of the manuscript.

Vincent J. Bertolini
Chicago, January 2000

THE EROTIC SIGN

Maria Rosa Cutrufelli

THE WORDS OF ANATOMY

Femininity is a "principle of uncertainty," Jean Baudrillard writes. "It causes the sexual poles to waver. It is not the pole opposed to masculinity, but what abolishes the differential opposition, and thus sexuality itself."[1]

Baudrillard's analysis is clear, straightforward, and consequential. "Freud was right," he writes, "there is but one sexuality, one libido—and it is masculine. Sexuality has a strong, discriminative structure centered on the phallus, castration, the Name-of-the-Father, and repression. There is none other. There is no use dreaming of some nonphallic, unlocked, unmarked sexuality. There is no use seeking, from within this structure, to have the feminine pass through to the other side, or to cross terms. Either the structure remains the same, with the female being entirely absorbed by the male, or else it collapses, and there is no longer either female or male—the degree zero of the structure."[2] And this means the "neutralization" of sex in the infinite potentialities of desire.

Women are mistaken, maintains Baudrillard, to refuse the true power of the feminine, which is the power of seduction. Men exert the power of sex through political logic and within the economic order. But "seduction represents mastery over the symbolic universe, while power represents *only* mastery of the real universe."[3]

If, therefore, "anatomy is destiny," and this equation is "phallic by definition,"[4] then women are doubly mistaken when, in rejecting the prisonhouse of anatomy, they haul the body into court. If the word of the body is the word woman, then the circle closes on itself, since once again we are in the realm of the anatomical word, once again imprisoned.

Baudrillard's position is, in all its clarity, very schematic. His argument is based on a simple binary logic: the body, in his view, is either a metaphor or a fate.

Other theories of subjectivity, born simultaneously with modern feminist political praxis, follow more complex structures, putting the body, sexuality, and language into strict relation with one another. Such theories, not accidentally, all finally converge on a common interest: writing, and in particular, on women's writing.

But what thread ties word and desire, sexuality and narrative, body and language in tight knots of interdependence? For the philosopher Rosi Braidotti, as for the semiotician Patrizia Violi, the body must not be understood as merely a biological or a sociological category, but rather as a point of overlap between "the physical, the symbolic, and the sociological." The body is, in short, "a surface of signification, situated at the intersection of the alleged facticity of anatomy with the symbolic dimension of language." To simplify: the self is always marked by gender (I-she, I-he); it is, so to speak, an incarnated structure that "finds a voice," becomes a subject, and, paradoxically, "becomes a corpus, is engendered" not in anatomy but in language. It is, therefore, language—and, consequently, representation—that is the site of the constitution of the subject.[5]

At the same time, as Teresa de Lauretis writes, it is certainly the case that "sexuality is the site upon which the subject elaborates its image of itself, its own corporeal awareness and knowledge, its modes of relating and acting in the world."[6] But sexuality is also the place of contradictions and ambivalences, of resistance and risk. Sexuality makes things problematic, precisely because it is the nodal point at which "instances of the corporeal, the psychic, and the social intertwine to constitute subjectivity and the limits of the self."[7]

Though at this point infinite avenues of inquiry open up, it is nevertheless clear why the question of language exerts such a charm upon feminist scholars. It is equally clear why sexuality presents itself as such a difficult and central theoretical node. It is through the enigmatic alchemy of body-sexuality-language that the dream of female freedom, of being and becoming a subject, of representing oneself as a subject, takes shape. The dream gains a dimension of reality when, at last, the word is translated into writing.

The true and proper passion of many women for the practices of writing has its origin here, in this process of construction and representation of oneself as a subject. But in this process sexuality plays an ambiguous role. Erotic desire and activity (which constitute the plot, the meshwork stretched upon the loom of sexuality) can be implosive, fragmenting, incoherent. Narrative, the literary account, often emphasizes the ostensibly triumphant subject's sensation of being eclipsed as it penetrates into the darker and more secret mazes, the more unexplored recesses of desire. But with what consequences?

"Eros is at work in all writing," writes the Canadian theorist Nicole Brossard.[8] And one immediately asks, what might this mean for women? To *which* body is Eros being here referred? *Which* body, *which* desire, *which* subject is passing through the writing?

This is a question one must inevitably pose in the long voyage of exploration toward sexuality. And one of the most arduous journeys is certainly the one that leads us into the "forbidden city" of erotic literature, which the writer Marisa Rusconi calls "virtually a scorched earth, without preexisting roots or sprouts."[9] Female erotic writing is an enterprise that, in order to achieve its fullest realization, requires many diverse voices and narrations, given the many different experiences each one of us carries with us and brings to bear along the way.

Which body, *which* desire, *which* subject—*which* sexuality? A question that has already received many answers, as many as there are stories authored by women, which with ever more frequency, using different (often radically different) means and forms, enter the gates of the "forbidden city," of the kingdom of Eros.

The Erotic Imaginary

Many women authors have tried to construct maps, to delimit borders. In these literary cartographies of sexuality and of erotic desire, experimentation is, for many such writers, the primary navigational tool. Austrian women writers perhaps most of all, Liesl Ujvary, Waltraud Anna Mitgutsch, Elfriede Jelinek, and others, have closely linked linguistic innovation— the subversion of traditional structures, even the rupture of grammatical conventions—to the theme of the erotic. Some have used a broken language, a distorted literary sign, to explore female eroticism. Others have instead sought new expressive means to unmask the "male gaze" upon the body of women. Elfriede Jelinek, in particular, proceeds by negation, using in her novels an imitative language drawn from magazines "for men" and from advertising. Her aim? "To reconquer the representation of the obscene and of nudity," a representational project "usurped by men to such an extent that no room remains for women to take up similar issues, and thus they are destined to fail if they try." Her own effort ultimately fails as well, as she herself admits, though it might be called "a constructive failure."[10] To proceed exclusively by negation cannot be effective: this strategy leaves the male gaze single and unitary, and male desire can still rule uncontested over the territory of Eros.

Jelinek's novels are "political," novels of denunciation. And yet, paradoxically, they were largely rejected by critics who accused them of being pornographic.

Obscenity, pornography, eroticism—the boundaries between these concepts are labile, subjective. They shift according to changing epochs, tastes, customs.

Angela Carter, who in her novels writes about the "mistresses of the whip," of female slaves and sadistic pleasures, shrewdly observes, "I believe that people find many different things erotic, and I find it difficult to generalize . . . Perhaps one characteristic of erotic literature, if I had to try to define it as a genre, is that of not taking sex for granted." Eroticism, generally speaking, "problematizes sex," while in pornography "sex is everywhere, in every form, is a consumer product that loses its value."[11]

Erotic literature, on the other hand, is precisely the exploration of the boundaries between the obscene and the erotic, between pornography and erotic art, between the great temptation and the great challenge. This play of stereotypes within the genre—what is masculine, what is feminine, what belongs to men, what to women—is conducted along a very fine edge and is always dangerously balanced between convention and transgression. But in life as in literature, all of our cards have now been shown, and the game is changed. Mere transformation is now all too obvious, in the relations between the sexes as in the relations between each individual and herself.

If we analyze the literary production of the last decades, we immediately see that excess and cruelty, violence, sadism and masochism are not exclusively (no longer?) marks of the male sexual imaginary. But for many female writers the question remains, does this yet again indicate some kind of mirroring, some mimesis of the masculine?

Angela Carter replies, "Female sexuality has been seen alternately as nonexistent or uncontainable, to be negated through the imposition of the value of virginity, or to be controlled through the practice of monogamy and through other forms of restriction. There has been a grand stereotipifying of female sexuality . . . Women in Western (and not solely Western) culture are represented as beings determined by sex, alternately obsessed by or alienated from their needs."

Stereotypes, clichés whose durability is based precisely on the undemonstrability of that which they assert. Women, it is said, more strictly equate sex with love, are more concerned with the emotional component of sex, have more pronounced difficulty separating feeling from the sexual relation. According to Carter, all this is an invention, or rather, a "cultural convention." For others, however, in this undoubted "historical invention" lies the germ of "difference," of a possible alternative route, not yet well delineated, ungraspable, and nevertheless present.

At this point, it is worth taking a step backward. There exists a cultural, philosophical, and literary tradition that has the "erotic eye" coincide with the "sadistic eye"—a masculine tradition par excellence.

Eroticism is a form of knowledge that writers and philosophers have from time to time tied to an idea of loss and of suffering, a feeling of dissipation, and a "strong" concept of power from which there is no escape. The erotic experience, wedded in this way to mystical experience, destroys reality at the very moment in which it discovers it. In his introduction to a well-known work of Georges Bataille, Alberto Moravia writes, "The sexual relation, like Attila, leaves no grass on the ground over which it passes. It creates desert around itself and calls that desert 'reality.'" Since it projects man outside of the world, the erotic experience is a devaluation and rejection of the world itself. And no return is ever possible, as Moravia writes: "The bridges are burned; the real world is lost forever."[12]

This grandiosely tragic vision of the power of sex is by no means unfamiliar to women. But there is a difference, the difference that for women, return is always possible. The cancel-

Maria Rosa Cutrufelli

lation of the world is never total, never definitive. Destructiveness is not an obsession. Alina Reyes, who achieved success in France with her first published work, an erotic tale, has explained with great simplicity: "Male eroticism is too enslaved to its ghosts, its stereotypical and repetitive fantasies, voyeuristic imaginings; at bottom, to abstractions. Women, instead, are more tied to the concrete experience of the flesh, to matter."[13]

Matter, flesh, the body, and the word that, in representing the body, in narrating desire, constructs a new subject, a subject of words who does not render her body a neutral potentiality, an undifferentiated sexual force. It is for this reason, perhaps, that female-authored erotic stories tend to be regarded as either simple "repositories of perversions" or pure "philosophies of sex." Such stories, quite to the contrary, move with grace or with power, with drama or with irony, through a kind of writing that draws not "one" sexuality (a fixed model, outside of time and history), but the various ways of living sex. Thus, contrary to what Baudrillard maintains, the infinite possibilities of desire can incarnate themselves in an "I," can find body and voice in a "subject."

In Italy, it is rare for women writers to dare to enter within the walls of the "forbidden city." We do not have, in contrast to other countries, our own actual tradition of female-authored erotic literature. Representations of eros and stories of sex, today as yesterday, remain on the margins of Italian women's writing. But the impression one gets is that, just under the surface, the swelling river of erotic narration is flowing, and at times bursts powerfully through. I am thinking about the cruel and tormented stories of Francesca Sanvitale (*La realtà è un dono: Racconti* [Reality Is a Gift: Stories]) as well as a previous novel that created scandal, *La ragazza di nome Giulio* [A Girl Called Jules] by Milena Milani.[14]

The authors in this anthology—the first of its kind in Italy—belong to different generations; they are quite diverse in their use of tone and narrative style, and diverse, too, in terms of the way that each understands eroticism. They represent individual women's voices that narrate and explore distant worlds, often quite alien to each other: the ancient temptations of sadomasochism, the close tie between amorous emotions and the emotions of sex, the elusive games of seduction. Sex, the raw sexual impulse, remaining at times in the background of these stories, is periodically invoked, and then returned to its simple function as a narrative expedient.

Different in intention—therefore, different in tone. But, having accepted the task of writing a story that was erotic "by design," all of the writers appearing in this anthology proved to have something in common: a relish for the challenge, a passion for delving.

Because, in the final analysis, *In the Forbidden City* is none other than this: a plumbing of the depths, an immersion—cautious or daring, enervating or vigorous—in the current, still subterranean, of "our" erotic narrative.

NOTES

1. Jean Baudrillard, *Seduction,* trans. Brian Singer (New York: St. Martin's Press, 1990), 12.

2. Ibid., 6.

3. Ibid., 8. Emphasis mine.

4. Ibid., 9.

5. Rosi Braidotti, *Nomadic Subjects* (New York: Columbia University Press, 1994), 198, 200–1, 238.

6. Teresa de Lauretis, "Irriducibilità del desiderio e cognizione del limite," paper presented at the conference "La soggettività femminile," held at the Salone del Libro in Turin, Italy, 17 May 1996.

7. Ibid.

8. Nicole Brossard, *The Aerial Letter,* trans. Marlene Wildeman (Toronto: The Women's Press, 1988), 83.

9. Marisa Rusconi, "L'immaginario erotico—passioni, piaceri, fantasie, seduzioni," *Tuttestorie,* vol. 1 no. 0 (March 1990).

10. Elfriede Jelinek, interviewed by Margit Knapp, *Tuttestorie,* vol. 1 no. 0 (March 1990).

11. Angela Carter, interviewed by Paola Bono, *Tuttestorie,* vol. 1 no. 0 (March 1990).

12. Georges Bataille, *Storia dell'occhio* (Rome: Gremese, 1991), preface by Alberto Moravia.

13. Alina Reyes, interviewed by Marisa Rusconi in *Tuttestorie,* vol. 1 no. 0 (March 1990).

14. Francesca Sanvitale, *La realtà è un dono. Racconti* (Milan: A. Mondadori, 1987). Milena Milani, *La ragazza di nome Giulio. Romanzo* (Milan: Longanesi, 1964), translated by Graham Snell as *A Girl Called Jules* (London: Hutchinson, 1966).

S I M E N A

Ippolita Avalli

Rome, October 14, 1996

Dearest Valerio,

Today I received a long missive from Alessia. Pages from a diary—dated August 12—that she wrote on Simena, apparently a few days prior to the awful deed. The letter only arrived today because the zip code was incorrect. The postmark from Istanbul is from a month ago. This means that it wandered from post office to post office before finally finding its way to me. I don't understand how Alessia could have forgotten my zip code. She knew it by heart. She was obsessive about memorizing numbers. The only way I can explain it to myself is by thinking that she must have done it on purpose, so that the letter would arrive much later. You see, Valerio, it is clear, however difficult to accept: Alessia had designed the entire thing in its most minute details. She was the one who provoked our separation on the island. The argument was a pretext so that she would be left alone. I don't feel guilty for not having searched for her. There was no way I could have imagined what she had in mind. I didn't even know that she kept a diary. In the few days that we were together I never saw her writing. I didn't find paper in her suitcase, nor did she have any on her that dreadful night in the ruins of the agora. Yes, it is terrible to admit that Alessia planned everything, because the question naturally arises: did she know that she was risking her life, or did she simply want to lose it? These pages are her artistic last will and testament. I've heard it said that literature is a pale metaphor of life. Alessia proves the contrary to be true. Was not what happened on Simena perhaps the corporeal dimension of her writing? She wrote first what she then lived. She must have given someone on the island the packet to send to me, afterward. She knew I would show it to you. If she wanted us to be her witnesses it was so that her quest for truth would not be lost, would not pass into silence. However questionable, it was genuine.

If you have the courage to give this diary to the authorities, they will probably grant Alessia's jailors the benefit of extenuating circumstances. They will believe Ahmet Güluk, who maintained that he was provoked and driven against his will to do what he did with or without accomplices. You will have to endure the scandal. But it is also true that this is the only way to render justice to your wife. You must never forget that Alessia knew exactly what she was doing.

But Valerio my dear, who was Alessia? I ask you because you've held her in your arms. You should know her. To know. Did she lie to us? Or was it simply that in your arms she also felt that she was not whole? Or that something of herself constantly escaped her, something that obstinately and innocently went in search because it could not resist doing so? What did she find over there—she was so insistent that we go to Turkey!—that extinguished the light and thickened the darkness?

In these pages Alessia is no longer that introverted and dreaming girl who avoided conflict and suffered at every minor disappointment. The words that she uses, how she uses them, have more than once roused the little animal residing between my legs (as she herself calls it). Reading, I seem to be able to feel her excited breath on my neck, to see her hands hurry under her skirt, and this has made me eager to satisfy myself with my own hands. Does this seem crazy to you? Immoral? I'm inclined to believe that Alessia wrote specifically to excite herself. She knew that for these purposes the word is a good deal more eloquent and poignant than images. She created a red thread of connection between herself and her assassins well before the one between us. I don't believe that her death was a tragic accident, as her aggressors claim. Rather, I think that at that point Alessia knew enough about herself to be able to set off the earthquake that would eradicate every shred of certainty in those boys, luring them down into the chasm into which she herself wished to plunge.

If the death of Alessia was agonizingly painful for you, it will be even more so now. Knowing her to be ignorant of herself, you could have continued to think of her with tenderness. Will you be able to sustain your love for her after having read? Will you ever find the strength to approach another woman without feeling like swooning with terror? I could have spared you, I know, but—forgive me—I cannot remain the sole guardian over her abyss, nor do I have sufficient strength to contain by myself the fear that lends the possibility of coming so near to life, to its source.

I know not what else to tell you, Valerio. Take care of yourself.

Luisa

SIMENA, SEPTEMBER 5, '96

The room is immersed in dusk. The girl is hanging by her wrists from a hook in the ceiling. She is completely naked and shines like a lamp. Her forms are perfect. The harmony of her proportions renders her beauty abstract, otherworldly. From her temple a line of blood descends that, from her chest, crosses her navel, her pubic hair, and drips into the void beneath. The room has no floor.

I am sitting on a swing that sways over the same void. From underneath, from the depths, from within—from where?—rises the fresh sound of a waterfall. Someone has grasped me behind the neck, is covering my mouth with a pillow. I can still see the woman with my eyes closed; she presses her lips together, an ineffable smile, gripped by an intense pleasure. Is it me? I ask myself. Is it me? I ask myself with joy because I feel like I am losing blood. I am not able to move my feet, my ankles hurt, something—a metal clamp? a rope?—is tying them together. Blows. I feel them resounding in my belly, then nothing. More blows. I have the sensation of coming up from the bottom of the sea. I rise, breathe, kick; the air splits my lungs. I open my eyes suddenly, awake, present. The swing is gone, so is the fresh sound of the waterfall. The room, the shabby mat, the tight ropes around my wrists and ankles: my present. Blows resound from outside, with the sounds of alternating male voices. They are fighting. Someone is throwing someone else out, who has no intention of leaving.

Are you searching for me, Luisa? Have you begun to comb the village, or have you decided that I can go to hell and washed your hands of me as soon as you could no longer explain my behavior to yourself? You could never imagine where I am at this moment. In a physical place certainly, but that is not what I mean. My *where* has become something else. In *this* where I know exactly where I am. From the moment I desired to know myself, everything changed. I have chosen silence, to be a placid boat that the wind pushes away from shore, so that nothing any longer remains of it, not even the shallow imprint of its keel upon the water.

I try to get up, but a sharp pain forces me back down upon the mat. My ankles bleed and ache, as does my chest, where I can feel deep scratches burning. The sheet is completely impregnated with the acrid odor of Ahmet's semen. It mixes with the sharp smell of dung coming from outside. There must be a chicken coop outside the window. Thin bands of light filter through the rolling shutter. It must be late afternoon, since the bay is echoing with the prolonged whistle of the last ferry. If I could, I would open the shutters at dusk, when the boats of the tourists round the harbor mouth and the few remaining are resting sun-burned in shady whitewashed rooms, or making love, or dining and conversing on catamarans left to rock lazily in the shallow water. Ahmet has not yet removed the bandages from my mouth. He doesn't know that I wouldn't scream, wouldn't call for help. I would never betray him, giving in to the temptation to speak a familiar language. What do I any longer have to share with a lover of the sea, a sun worshipper? I belong now to another race. What was before— or, outside of this room, could still be—no longer interests me. If I write to you, Luisa, it is because without witnesses things do not exist. Or perhaps I still need to hold open a gap in that wall that by now separates me from what was our world. Now my world is the cock of Ahmet, its thrusts. The world of my pleasure is this room whose world is this house, and that of the house is the village that contains it, and of the village the promontory, the millenary outcropping of Simena and Kekova, the island that faces it.

How long is it that I've been here? Two, three days? It's not important to know, I must not be interested, I tell myself. And yet, thinking of you still here in the village gives me strength, helps me force the boundary a little further beyond, helps me descend ever more deeply into myself. I made a discovery. If you no longer fear it, pain becomes a lamp that lights your way and calls with siren song: over here, over here.

While he ties me up and then fucks me, he watches me. He never takes his eyes off me, and neither do I. What is he looking for in my eyes as he forces his way into my vagina?

What do I search for in his eyes while he binds my wrists? While he beats me? I believe it is the same thing, and this excites me: his permission. That he give me permission to be there where his cock reaches me. The bluish marks left by the bindings, rough cords taken from the boats, move us to tenderness as if born of our love. Before leaving he loosens them. He reverently kisses the wounds. After he leaves, the solitude doesn't weigh on me, doesn't frighten me the way it used to. When I used to be unable to be alone, I would be with anyone in order to be with someone. I drag myself to the spot beneath the window and brace myself against the wall, trying to stand up. I'm up, and this gives me a certain sense of arrogance, as if having stood up I had called the room around me into being. What I am today depended on last night. What I will be tomorrow, on this night that is coming to an end.

I know that if I am still alive it is because he likes to fuck me and watch me while he fucks me—it is the dead who no longer see. He pushes me up against the wall, he puts his hands between my legs and finds me wet. This enrages him. He forces my teeth open with his fingers in order to show me who is in charge. He forces me to my knees and gives it to me to suck, and I do. My knee trembles like a fly beating against the pane of a closed window, but I can't stop it. He knows that I want it, I like it that he pushes in and out of my mouth at his own pleasure, that he comes in my mouth without caring at all about me, how many times he wants me to fellate him again, blow job yes, suck—(I bet that the animal between your legs has begun to quiver, Luisa, am I right?)—the room, the walls, the objects, all the objects in the world, the whole world has exploded, the pieces blown into the air and now sailing into silence, descending quietly into silence like the semen of Ahmet burning my throat, almost as if their descent lasted unto eternity. From the moment that Ahmet fucks me while watching me nothing will ever again return to its place—the pieces will not fuse back together into their original structure, nor will I be able to make them.

It happened very suddenly. But it must have always been ready in me. I awakened in the workers at the excavation site that particular interest evoked by mad women, reckless women, women who when they walk give the sensation of bodily surrender, of a nostalgia in the spine. Their tongues licked around their lips, they whistled after us: "Madame Odeon! Madame Sebasteion!" I snapped my fingers at them. What are you doing?—you said, appalled—they're not dogs! If you had not been there, I would have let myself fall to the ground, the sand would have welcomed my body, I would have opened my legs, my arms, my mouths, and the ring of my sphincter. Prone and obedient, I would have happily surrendered to their intrusion. If you had not been there. You never understood why I broke into tears when—laughing—one of the workers suddenly poured a goatskin full of water on me.

Seated in the shade of a patio picking out carpets, our being together was still a reality. But now my tears, more than the water from the goatskin, had revealed my truth to me. Those nameless boys were more precious to me than you and all our conversations. Do you understand what I'm trying to tell you? My wet dress had stuck to me, displaying the gentle swelling with the cleft in the middle, the one between my legs. There beats my only heart. From the moment the excavator poured the goatskin out on me I began to exist. The eyes of the prisoner fill with tears of joy at the prospect of the next liberation.

Indecent. Fabric that traces out an empty crack where the captured gaze loses itself.

I trembled. But my trembling didn't frighten me because it proclaimed my happiness. It revealed my true face to me, it demonstrated my easy consistency. An urgent desire to rip the fabric from between my legs, to be naked, to give myself over once and for all. They laughed. You laughed, too.

You didn't see the one boy drop his shovel.

For years now you have been my best friend. I've always wanted to be like you. If you gained weight, I gained weight too. If you were thin, so was I. What I loved about you grew so gigantic in me, without my wanting it to, that it took up the space of an entire day. You asked me, "What do you dream of?" Only now am I able to give you a meaningful answer. I dream of being filled up, everywhere, at once. I know that it would never be enough. The more Ahmet gives me, the more I feel the lack of it. But this is not his fault; the lack is in me. He only brings it to existence. He gives it body.

I seem to hear you ask, why do you say this? And Valerio? Do you no longer love him? Valerio. We got engaged at fifteen years old. I believe he fell in love with me because I slammed his hand in the drawer of my father's desk when he deflowered me without looking at me.

Food made me sick, I felt it, and yet I couldn't help but constantly swallow something. Then I would vomit. It would make space in my stomach to fill with something else, that something from which I would immediately liberate myself. My entire girlhood and all the years of marriage went on like this.

Above me Valerio was panting hard, alone and unreachable. I locked my thighs, squeezing him tightly, but to whom did I want to prove that I was there? That Valerio was pressing heavily down upon me comforted me, like coming home after a long day of work and traffic, kicking off your shoes, and flopping onto the couch.

Valerio shifted his head to the side and watched me. He was careful not to assume an expression of disapproval or disappointment. Was I making love with him, or not? He was always about to ask me that, but he never did. He preferred to finish up quickly, before the sadness finally caught up with him. Afterward, we gave each other a slight kiss on the cheek. I should never have corresponded with him, I know, but I couldn't help it. I was unable to tell him anything. I loved him so much that he became invisible to me. Love hid him from me.

He would roll his large body onto the mattress, away from me. I would not move. I would begin to wait, with my whole being. I closed my eyes. In the darkness I heard the bedsprings squeak, "What am I going to do with you, what am I going to do . . ." I would hear him murmur. I waited full of hope, ready to seize his hand. It could have all begun at that point. But Valerio never even tried to scratch at the wall that separated us. He would get up, I would hear him make his way to the bathroom. The light would immediately filter from under the door, the water would gurgle in the sink. I would remain prisoner of that small bit of stuff of which each of us— if abandoned to ourselves—is made.

I would hurriedly get dressed. I wanted to be ready before he came out of the bathroom, to preserve for myself the illusion that nothing had occurred so that everything could still happen.

It is true: women are strong and crazy enough to keep lit, beyond any reasonable doubt, the flame of hope.

He placed two chairs together back to back. He made me sit on the first, tying my ankles to the legs of the chair. Then he made me arch backward and extend my arms over my head. He tied my wrists to the legs of the other chair. The position is terribly uncomfortable, and Ahmet beats me pitilessly on my abdomen, on my breasts. He uses a thin switch so as to be able to beat me even more, making my skin redden before it splits and begins to bleed.

The muscles of my legs and arms, my carotid artery, are

pulled so taut they seem about to snap. My back pulsates. I begin to cry. Tears run freely; I do nothing to hold them back. I cry like one who has lost everything. I beg him, I implore him, though I only speak to him in my head, I am too ashamed to use my tongue because Ahmet does not understand. To come to myself I must adhere to him, never be separated from him. Ahmet is watching me in silence from some place within the room. He approaches me from behind and rips the bandage off my mouth. He shoves his cock in down to its root and remains immobile. His flesh is suffocating me, it is the end, I think, to save myself I cleave to his flesh, I suck it and suck it, and slowly the spasms of fear dwindle, my stomach muscles unclench, my tears subside. I continue to suck it filled with thankfulness until I feel it empty itself completely into my mouth. He pulls out of me and covers my mouth again with the bandage. The pain begins again, stronger this time. I whimper. I moan. My kidneys are burning, the room is filled with the pulsations of my temples. Ahmet removes my bindings from the chair legs but leaves my wrists and ankles tied together. I crumple onto the mat. He watches me from the doorway, and by the look in his eyes I am able to tell that he knows the secret of my happiness.

If Ahmet were to say a word, a single word—I mean, a word having to do with us, the word of our desire—the stones of which the territory around us is made would shatter into fragments, and a tongue of fire would swallow the promontory and dry up the Mediterranean Sea.

One afternoon, a few days before leaving, I went to the pond. Two wild ducks made a great commotion coming out of the bushes. I got undressed in the little cove where we always undressed. The afternoon work was beginning in the fields opposite, and soon the din of the farm equipment would fracture the silence that we love so well. I jumped in carrying a life preserver since I don't know how to swim very well. From that distance I looked back at the place that I had occupied on the shore. The towel spread out, the tube of sunscreen, the book opened to the page I had been reading. I imagined Valerio coming out of the bushes and finding my things there without me. Where was I? Disappeared. Kidnapped. From what? From whom? The water suddenly became colder. I swam with large strokes. I got back to the shore completely out of breath, with my heart exploding in my chest. The life preserver remained floating out in the middle of the pond. It gently bobbed. What of me had I left out there forever? What erases me, what makes me vanish as soon as Ahmet approaches me? With him I feel relieved of the tremendous weight of being a woman. Departing from my body, everything loses body.

Ahmet helps me rise to my feet. It is painful for me to walk. And yet I do not know my own flesh except those places where he has lacerated it. I hesitate for a moment when I realize I am being taken outside. Contact with the fresh air disorients me. Ahmet understands this, and he quickly removes the scarf he wears tied around his head and places it upon my eyes. He ties it at the nape of my neck and guides me forward, holding me by the knot as if I were a workhorse, a mare. We walk upon the flat undergrowth of a footpath, and every time my knees give way Ahmet yanks me upright, beats me. The scent of his sweaty skin makes my head spin. We are going uphill. I remember having seen the ruins of a castle at the summit of the promontory. For a second I think that I might run into you, and I begin to panic. But I tell myself that you wouldn't be able to recognize me. Not anymore.

I don't know where Ahmet is leading me and I can't ask him. Questions have no relevance to the way we understand each other; they are extraneous, he would be truly unable to understand me. And I have nothing to ask, anyway. When I fall again, other hands raise me up. There must be three of them, maybe four. Boys from the neighborhood. Someone hoists me up like a young goat on his shoulders. A hand clamps my buttocks. Fingers playing along the waistline of my skirt slide under the elastic of my panties and forage in my pubic hair. They follow the groove between my buttocks down to my anus and caress its ring. Other fingers make their way between the lips of my sex and plunge unceasingly inside me. An entire hand penetrates me with force up to the wrist. I kick and squirm, but it's no use: I remain impaled. Another hand under my tee shirt finds my nipples. As soon as it grazes them they harden. The hand freezes, surprised. My excitement is so apparent that they quickly decide. They depart immediately from me. The sensation of emptiness that I feel is sudden and unbearable. I would prefer bodily torture to this void that freezes my blood, this emptiness in my innards that makes me writhe and whine. I am put down. Sharp stones hurt the soles of my feet, my back. They have placed me against a rugged boulder. Then they rip off my gag. One gives me his tongue to suck while another fucks me standing up and another squeezes my nipples. As soon as he sticks it in, the one who is fucking me comes. This sends him into a rage. He becomes insane. He strikes out at me blindly. He insults me. I was not ready to hear these voices. I cry; the blindfold soaks up my tears. Another mounts me. He makes me spread me legs widely so he can stick it in as far as possible. Ahmet—his touch I recognize—fondles my buttocks as if waiting for it to get as big and hard as possible before he in turn slips it inside me. They fuck me simultaneously, from the front and the back; they stick it in my mouth, in my hands, between my breasts, under my armpits, in my eyes, against the soles of my feet, the back of my neck; and all the while they beat me and beat me without ever ceasing to thrust, they pound me with dismay and resignation, coming inside, below, above, upon me to the last drop.

I return to consciousness feeling a strange lightness. I've lost the blindfold, and I can see them between my swollen eyelids.

Ippolita Avalli

They move off along the footpath stumbling, jostling each other, dark-haired boys of incredible beauty. I am bleeding from the mouth, from my breasts. I have difficulty moving my right arm. I can't feel my legs, and a nervous tic makes my eyelid flutter. Using my shoulder as a support, I roll myself over onto my back. Semen runs from between my legs, from my eyelashes, my mouth, my sphincter. It clots in my hair, on my hands. The sparkling morning air strokes me, and in the slice of sky I can see the stars are fading rapidly into daybreak. I would sing if my throat weren't full of blood.

With a final effort, of which I would never have believed myself capable, I arch my lower back, then shift my weight up and onto my legs. Wavering, I grasp a stone with one hand and heave myself forward and down upon my chest. I see down below me a shining sarcophagus, tiny in the immensity of ocean that was once a vast plain. From some place around the promontory I hear the motor of a boat putting out to sea. The crowing of the roosters greets the day. The rattle of shutters opening echoes among the stones.

A little boy comes out of a shack and runs along the crest of a hill lying below. He is naked from the waist down under a tattered tee shirt. He stops for a moment uncertainly, as if compelled by some force, and looks up. He sees the strange being upon her knees, gripping a massive boulder. He cannot understand that he is seeing a woman with a mangled throat who beams in ecstasy. He quickly detaches his gaze from her and takes off running again, disappearing behind a garden wall.

Years Later

Angela Bianchini

The girl was dressed all in white: her angora sweater, white; her low-cut silk blouse, white, but spattered with rain and mud; her skirt long, pleated. The only article of clothing appropriate for that inclement winter day, her clunky black shoes; they had no laces, however, and looked like they were full of water.

When she saw her, framed in the sidelight of the front door, the first impulse of the woman was one of compassion: "Poor dear, in this nasty weather!"

Then, in a split second, she realized that she had been completely wrong: the girl seemed perfectly fine. She had dressed that way by her own free will, to use one of those clichéd expressions that the woman, who had been a journalist and who believed she was very knowledgeable about language, found simply detestable.

Of *her* own personal choice—that is, to employ someone unknown, someone recommended to her by mere acquaintances to help her draft the book she intended to write, and she not yet knowing whether it would take the form of a memoir, a novel, or short stories—she now had even greater doubts, especially upon seeing the girl for the first time. From the very beginning she had thought she would do all the work herself, as had been her practice. But precisely because she had always done it herself, and now being retired, she wasn't sure she could pull it off. Of self-indulgence, to be sure, she had barely had experience, and she knew nothing of the art of carving out time to dedicate entirely to herself during the long days that she now had available to her. Working at the computer for her, though, was just work, not pleasure. There remained, moreover, unresolved and fundamental, the problem of how to write these reminiscences or sketches or whatnot of hers: whether in the first or the third person. For days, for months now, she had recounted them to herself as they came naturally to her, that is, in the first person. But she felt that they were too much her own, too personal, too full of her actual feelings to submit to an editor or an audience, presuming that some day or other things should arrive at such a pass.

Then, in a flash, without her having expected it, or rather, when she had simply lost all hope and had decided to shelve the project, she managed, by some miracle, to see and to speak of herself as if doubled: to narrate a someone no longer she, but one who moved and thought as she did and had lived the same experiences.

And then, thrilled, empowered in a way that she could never have imagined herself to be, she began to jot down, in objective form, the many stories, the many episodes of her life; and the further along she got the easier, in a certain sense, it became. The style she found difficult, but she effortlessly observed from afar the little girl born in the late twenties and reaching adolescence before the war, in an age that seemed both extremely near and remote at the same time.

Out of all this came an extremely labored manuscript, full of marginal notes that, once fully copied out, she had managed to render on the page as clearly as she possibly could. And of this text written out by hand with great care, she tried to speak, a little out of breath, to the girl, whose name was Sandra, in the short hallway between the vestibule and the little study.

"I just need to be able to read it."

The observation rang as a rebuke of the woman's eccentricity. In the meantime, the girl had sat down at the laptop, opened it, and was looking at it in a professional manner, waiting.

"It will take a lot of time to make it out," she then commented discerningly, having taken a quick glance at the manuscript pages.

"That makes no difference to me. Do you have a lot of assignments?"

"No."

From that point on, she barely said another word, sitting bolt upright in the white blouse that exposed her neck and fragile, almost adolescent shoulders, on which the traces of a summer tan lingered, this too a silent rebuke of the gray, dusty light in the room.

"It's so hot in this house," she commented, pulling off her white sweater.

Her breasts were small under the white silk, her body in good shape, however muffled in the robes of her almost regal ensemble. Over the entire spectacle she presented hung the palpable air of oppressed and imperious youth, ever on guard.

Full of annoyance and scorn, but also a feeling of impotence, the woman began to search for a way to rid herself of the girl. This was not going to be easy, given that she had already imprudently let her in. However, any rudeness or impatience on Sandra's part, or, better still, any difficulty in deciphering her handwriting, could suffice as pretext for breaking off the relationship without undue ugliness, and for telling her, politely, in the woman's own style, how things stood, that perhaps it would be better not to go on, and that she would call her again some other time.

But the opportunity never arose. The girl began to calmly type, seemingly unbothered by anything. She typed quickly, and quite capably followed the written directions and marginalia in the text. She never asked questions, never seemed to require clarifications. She did not have the slightest curiosity about what she was reading. It was as if the scenes and years evoked by the woman had no further importance beyond that which the author attributed to them. It was as if, therefore, they went completely over her head, invisible, nonexistent, significant only in the terms that the woman herself had in mind and to which Sandra was entirely indifferent.

It was the woman who paced back and forth in the apartment, continually entering and reentering the studio so as to cast a glance at the computer and on the manuscript and see how far the girl had gotten. And it was she who was to give in first.

"Maybe you're a bit tired now. Also, I have to go out today. We can finish another day."

Yet again, she expected some reaction, a question maybe, some curiosity about what her work as a journalist had actually been like. It never came.

Sandra turned off the computer, lowered the lid, and got up. "When should I come back?"

"Not tomorrow," the woman weakly said; it seemed to her as if she had exerted a huge amount of energy that day. "Maybe the day after tomorrow. Are you busy?"

"The day after tomorrow," Sandra pronounced and, agile, fleet, grabbed her angora sweater, strode to the door, and headed out into the rain.

Afterward, the woman realized with satisfaction that the pages typed, and very accurately, by Sandra were not in fact formless, but more and more resembled a novel. The desire to write about herself had not been new, even if she had only recently become aware of the sensation of having had a life that was interesting, and even dense, however unknown to most. For many years she had been convinced that she too

Angela Bianchini

would ultimately wind up getting married, as had most women of her age. But such had not been the case. This was due to the fact that many of her love affairs had remained secret ones, generally by the preference of men who were all more or less happily married, or at any rate who were determined not to divorce, but who, however, required her anonymity. Undisclosed and private had also remained many beautiful and romantic moments of these love affairs: fleeting encounters, trips taken together, risky coincidences. And people had formed a certain image of her, she was sure, that was completely negative: dim, pale, a lonely woman devoid of passion. At this point in her life, and in a society in which everyone felt the need to relate their own experiences, this sense of her own obscurity weighed on her much more than her loneliness. She would disappear in silence, she sometimes told herself, carrying with her the secret of a life still hidden behind the discretion, by now become uncomfortable, of a proper older woman.

"Should I leave breaks?" Sandra asked on the second day.

"What do you mean, breaks?" The woman was immediately irritated by the question.

"Um, I don't know. Between one piece and another."

"They are chapters of a story."

The girl didn't move a muscle: "You tell me."

The week wore on like this, marked by the weariness of the woman and her desire for escape—from the presence of Sandra. She, Sandra, continued to have so few other commitments that the question arose as to how she managed to support herself, even to eat. But the woman had ceased wondering about it, since at her few timid inquiries Sandra had responded in a way that was not only terse but contradictory: one day it seemed as if she had family, the next as if she lived alone. Sometimes, carrying some sociology textbook, she gave the impression that she was studying for some scholarship competition or university exam, but on other occasions in the place of books appeared women's magazines or gossip sheets. Everything crammed into a bulging backpack hanging from those skinny shoulders that, at the moment of takeoff, was transformed into the motor that propelled that mysterious personality.

After the first part, dedicated to her childhood before the war, which was less boring, so it seemed to the woman, than many others, and narrated with remarkable brio, came the pages about the protagonist's adolescence, passed during the height of the war, with the young men leaving for the front, the first returning dead, the defeats, the bombardments.

"Here is the manuscript," she said to Sandra one morning.

She wondered if the girl would display any interest or curiosity. She merely asked for an explanation or two, and typed everything, names, initials, bombardments, arrests, the fall of fascism, with perfect equanimity, as if it all regarded some prehistoric epoch or archeological discovery and had nothing whatsoever to do with her.

"Here you are," she said. "You better check it over, to be sure."

"Come back in a day or two," the woman said. "I'll need some time."

In reality, she only needed to decide whether or not to entrust the pages that followed to Sandra. She delayed at great length, then, as usual, opted yet again for Sandra's presence. The pages had to do with the most intimate part of her life, and, in a certain way, she didn't want to entrust it to anyone. But, once she had decided that her novel was destined to be read, why exclude Sandra, who was a reader, indeed, but perhaps of the kind most indifferent and resistant to emotions?

"There are very few pages," she said to Sandra. "Today you will finish quickly."

Then, uneasy, she was unable to leave the room. She stayed there, in a corner, to follow through Sandra's work, through the fingers moving across the keyboard, the encounter so miraculously revived.

Angela Bianchini

Herself, to begin with: as a young girl at the time, very young, evacuated from Turin with her mother in 1944 into the Canavese area. Her mother maintains communication links with the partisans via a clandestine telephone hidden in a chest of drawers, and allows the girl, not without trepidation, to do her part as well, circulating from one town to another by bicycle carrying letters and provisions.

And the order one day to travel farther afield up into the mountains to meet with a particular partisan. Also scheduled to be there, a famous commander, renowned for his courageous actions and held in high repute The girl knows him only by his battle name: Stone. The arrival in the small house, almost a mountain hut, on a March day at dusk. All around her the snow, the cold, the last rays of sun on the mountaintops. The discovery that she is alone, for the time being, because she's arrived first, and the fear of having to spend the night by herself if something should prevent the others from arriving. And in the uninhabited house, a second discovery: a single bed with two blankets on it. And the long wait, as it begins to get dark.

Then, footsteps outside the hut. It is Stone, and only Stone. The other person will not be there, but Stone came, to make contact with her. Stone, with his magnetic presence, his fame. He lights a fire with some kindling, expresses concern for and interest in her young age, offers explanations, reassures her. With his mere presence he is able to make the hut habitable and the hour magic, even the darkness, the cold, the isolation. He wards off the anxieties, the danger. And she now finds herself at the very center of the little house, the object of Stone's attentions, seated in front of him as they consume their provisions.

Above the supper, meager and brief, above the conversation, Stone's questions, the answers, almost confessions, of the girl, Turin, the evacuation, her mother awaiting her return down in the valley, the little flirtation begun, almost as a joke, with the young man now a prisoner in Germany—above all of this hung the tangible apprehension of what was going to happen later, after the dinner was over.

And then, to find herself for the first time alone with a man who clearly desires her. The hands of Stone, so deft in their ability to unbutton a sweater or two, both necessary on account of the cold, and in the slipping off of undergarments: always delicate and deliberate in their movements, reassuring her that nothing will happen that she doesn't wish to, no step will be taken to which she doesn't consent. And, step by step, silent consent after consent, tenderness offered as if in compensation for her being a woman, and so young, defenseless, and brave, the girl is now beside him. Two bodies are near and know each other. It is no longer cold; the frost and the dangers are now shut outside, in the mountains, in the snow.

And there is also the girl's daring of herself, her hovering on the point of abandoning herself in a game completely new to her, which renders her potent and extremely desirable and which she knows that she can bring to an end from one moment to the next. And there is the occurrence of non-occurring, and her not wanting to surrender because she feels that the temptation is too great for her and what she would want most of all is to surrender.

And he who, without demanding, always asking, with infinite tenderness, draws even nearer to her, and she, acquiescing in almost everything. And he teaches her an extraordinary lesson in love: the hands, the body, his tongue, animal-like, coarse, but in reality most sweet—these things reveal her to herself, they reveal her own body to her, and his body, the immensity of unknown passages and landscapes, the depths of winding ravines and pathways that, as one descends, grow so gigantic they occupy all consciousness and will.

And then, after the exhausted slumber of a night that seemed everlasting, the awakening, still completely drenched in love and in the certainty that happiness waits just around the corner to be grasped at any moment. And instead, in the deserted mountain hideaway, the rosy reflection off the snow shining through the windowpanes, and a brief note leaned against a half-empty water jug: "What a shame. Until we meet again."

When she arrived at the end, Sandra raised her head. She had typed quickly, as usual, but made a few errors, and now went back to check and correct.

She said, "Did you ever see him again?"

Without even realizing it, automatically, the woman replied, "Only from afar. At a conference now and then."

Sandra shook her head, one could not tell whether out of sympathy or disdain. But, in a voice almost kind, she said: "What a shame."

From that point on, the relationship between Sandra and the woman was again changed. As the woman became more hesitant to give her more pages to type, Sandra became infinitely more attentive and lively, almost overeager.

"I'm sorry," she said a few days later, "tomorrow I can't come. Nor the day after. You will have to make appointments in advance now because I have another job."

"Really?" The woman felt instantaneous relief. "Is it work that you like? What does it involve?"

"It's with another journalist."

"Really?" repeated the woman, almost incredulously. "Maybe I know him. What's his name?"

The girl said the name. It was Stone.

The woman felt, in that very moment, that it was necessary to definitively rid herself of Sandra. All she needed to do was tell her, without offering any further explanation, that she no longer had any time to work on the project. But she did not do it that day, for fear of its seeming like some kind of retaliation, and she promised herself that she would call the girl or send a note.

Instead, she wound up not even doing that, and not having communicated with the girl in any way, she again found herself face-to-face with her. Only a few days had passed. Sandra, however, was completely changed. Instead of the usual long skirts, baggy and hanging, she was now wearing a black stretch miniskirt that showed off long, gorgeous legs that had until then always remained hidden. Her sweater, in a mottled pattern of gray and black, was also beautiful, as was her elegant, close-fitting leather jacket.

All this could have been completely new, or simply held in reserve prior to this moment. Sandra certainly seemed to be another person: older, thought the woman, observing with some satisfaction the wrinkles that appeared under the make-up, which itself had hitherto gone entirely unnoticed.

The details of the new job were conveyed directly to her by the girl, unusually talkative that day. She got along extremely well at the journalist's; she needed to go there every day, as it turned out, since there was so much work to do; and he was so happy to have her collaborating with him.

"And what are you writing together?" asked the woman. "Articles, letters?"

"Oh no. He, too, is writing his memoirs. A very interesting life."

Her intention to be hurtful was so apparent that the woman began to wonder if Sandra were not making it all up: the job, the journalist, the memoirs. But the details she described could surely only have been gotten firsthand, since they coincided not only with what was known publicly about Stone, who had become over the years quite a celebrity, but with certain intimate episodes known only among common friends and within small circles.

"How is he feeling these days?" the woman asked.

"Pretty well. But his eyesight is not so good. That is why he needs someone to help him write, and who can then read it back to him and help him correct it."

It was true, it was all true, and the image of a Sandra concerned and assiduously involved, such as the woman had never seen her, became plausible as well.

Angela Bianchini

"I imagine he needs the help of his wife quite a bit," the woman tried yet again, putting Sandra to the test.

"His wife? She was really sick, and she died a year ago." Sandra seemed almost shocked at the woman's ignorance.

This too was true. Stone had married a comrade from the Resistance, a bit older than himself, and with whom he had lived, from what one heard, perfectly happily. But now he was truly alone. Alone and in need of affection.

The woman sighed. It had all come full circle. Sandra had managed not only to destroy her image of the young Stone, but her image of herself. After her brief moment of creativity, she had returned to being the elderly woman with the pallid, spent life that she appeared to everyone else to be. The page containing that unique and extraordinary night still existed, but now she had no idea to whom to entrust it.

"Well, Sandra," the woman said, "I can see that from now on you will be quite busy. I too have a lot to do. Perhaps it would be best for us to discontinue our work."

"Yes," said Sandra, smiling cordially. "That would be best. The journalist is about to leave."

"Ah, yes?" The woman at that point had the feeling that she no longer understood what was going on. "So?"

"I'm going with him."

LIKE A BANANA

Rossana Campo

So, like, this is how the whole story happened. I'm hanging out with Ant and we run into Nunzi in front of Gino's bar, around by the school. I don't get how we're still always hanging around over there, now that *that* pain in the ass is over and all, at least for a while.

Anyway, I see Nunzi with Tony, who's her boyfriend, this month's boyfriend I mean, Nunzi who's had so many of them that we lost count. Whatever. And she, Nunzi, stops and she says to me: So, listen, I'm sorry, I'm really sorry, I know it's been a while that we haven't hung out, but I swear I felt like shit when I saw that they flunked you like that. Didn't I, Tony? didn't I feel like shit? But Tony just shrugs his shoulders and sucks on the filter of his Kool and says: how am I supposed to know?

So Nunzi rolls her eyes and then bends her leg like she's going to knee him right in the balls, but Tony's too quick and he jumps back before she can do it.

You saved your package this time, goes Ant, and she laughs. Nunzi, though, is too pissed, and she lights a cig and wipes lipstick from the corner of her mouth.

So, I'm sorry that they flunked you too, Nunzi, I go, I was really sorry, I swear.

I don't give a shit, Nunzi goes, I'm used to it. Come on, let's go get a beer, she goes, nodding her head toward Gino's shithole of a bar.

Tony is looking at Nunzi and he goes: I'm going to Enzo's, I'll catch you later.

But she acts like she wouldn't even bother to wipe her ass with him, she's so totally cool with guys; she makes them dance like they're walking on tacks, you should see her. So we sit down out front and Ant, who's one of those I-wish-I-could-but-I-can't types, starts checking out Nunzi with that retard's look on her face, and she goes from her gold thong sandals, with those red-painted toenails, to her totally tight faded Fiorucci's, then to her studded belt, and up to her almost see-through white tee shirt that she wears without a bra or anything, with the red lettering on it that says: OUT OF MY WAY—I'M PREGNANT.

Nunzi goes: Finished checking me out? God, what a pain she is!

Ant goes: That tee shirt is excellent! I'm pregnant! I've got to get me one of those tee shirts, too.

Give it up some time, I say, so people will believe you.

Did you go to Sicily? Ant asks Nunzi, damn, you are so tan! Did you know that Claudia can't go to the beach, can't swim, can't do nothing?

Why?

Uh, she caught a little you-know-what in her box, goes Ant, who loves it when she gets the opportunity to talk about someone behind her back.

No, come on, goes Nunzi.

It's true, Ant and I say at the same time.

And where did she get it, in church? goes Nunzi.

Yeah, right, in friggin' church! says Ant. Did you know that Claudia was going out with a guy who is in the service down in Diano?

When?

As soon as school was out. Her folks were letting her go out on Saturday night because she got her diploma, and she gave it up right away.

She is too stupid! goes Nunzi.

You never caught anything in your box, did you Nunzi?

Don't even . . . ! goes Nunzi, pointing the sign of the horns with her two fingers over at Ant, this chick is going to jinx me . . .

And Tony! You got a big crush on Tony, didn't you? Come on, you guys must be going out for like three months now. If you ask me, you got a totally massive crush on him.

Well, goes Nunzi, he knows how to do it too good, Tony does. Then she turns toward the bar and shouts: Hey, Gino baby, bring us three beers, would ya, we're so thirsty. Then she turns back to us and says: And you two! what the hell are you two always wandering around like two bums for, in all this heat. Why don't you find someone with a motorcycle that you can ride with . . .

Ant looks over at me and I try to stop her cold with a look. She never picks up on anything, she goes. Come on, let's tell her.

There ain't shit to tell her, I go.

Oh come on, Nunzi always tells us about all the nasty stuff she does all over town.

What have you two been up to?

Gino comes with the beers, and he goes: Yo, what are you all always around here for? You ain't going to the beach?

You know how it is, we've got a lot of important business around here, goes Nunzi, and she winks.

I try to change the subject, but Nunzi goes: Hold up, let me light a cigarette. She blows out a cloud of smoke and says: Now you have to talk.

I go: It's no big deal. It's like, one day there wasn't anyone around, not even a dog. This retard here went out with her mother, so I go for a walk down by the park, and Rino showed up on his motorcycle.

Rino . . . RINO??

Yeah, yeah, it was him, goes Ant.

Damn! He is so gorgeous! goes Nunzi, licking her chops.

She's had a crush on him since the ninth grade, says Ant, who minds everybody else's business but her own. She like fell for him right away. She says she even dreamed about him one night. Do you remember when he used to come and wait for Eva at the back door of the school?

Who could ever forget that? goes Nunzi, with her eyes twinkling. He used to sit there crosswise on his motorcycle. God, he looked so delicious I could eat him for breakfast.

Well, anyway, so he stops there on his motorcycle and he starts laughing, and I say: What the hell is so funny? And he goes: You have a chocolate moustache. Did you eat some chocolate?

God, how embarrassing . . . you two are always so embarrassing. I knew it, what a waste. I don't want to be seen any more hanging around with the likes of *you* two, goes Nunzi.

Then that's it. I'm not telling you, I go. Nunzi is one of those people who can be a big pain in the butt. She can be totally cool and all, and she's been doing it since the ninth grade, but I could slap her silly sometimes, I swear.

Oh no, now I want to hear the whole story. If he ragged on you a little you deserved it, so I give him a hand.

Can I go on? So he busts my chops about the chocolate, and then we chitchat for awhile . . .

Tell her what you said to him then, go on, goes Ant, bugging the hell out of me as usual.

So like I go: I'm not a kid, you know, who goes around all day eating candy and getting it all over her face. I just had a rocky road ice cream, is that OK with you?

Damn. You told him! So who cares, right? Come on, what else happened? goes Nunzi, all impatient.

He parks his motorcycle, and he says that I really made him want to get some ice cream, and would I go with him so that he can get some somewhere.

And you went for it, right then and there, I hope, goes Nunzi, demonstrating her belief that when it comes to certain things you don't need to think twice.

Yeah, yeah, I go.

No you didn't. First you lied to him. You said that you were waiting for me, goes Ant.

OK. First I lied to him. I go: I can't come with you because I'm waiting for Ant. But he goes: So, let's go get the ice cream, and then we'll sit here on this bench and we'll wait for her together. So I go: OK. And I go with him, and we have to walk for awhile because everything's closed, and there's not a fucking soul around anyway. It was like two o'clock and we were dying of heat.

And then?

And then we went back by the motorcycle and sat down to wait for Ant, for pretend, right? You get it?

Thanks. No I didn't get it, goes Nunzi. And Eva, that slut, where did he leave her?

I asked him the same thing, and he didn't say that much. He said that she went to work at some summer resort. She's a waitress somewhere.

Ha, ha, I love it! She's always so stuck-up, and now she's working as a waitress. That's too sweet, goes the evil Nunzi.

Tell her about when he kissed you, goes Ant, squirming around in her seat.

Can I tell it? Thank you! So like he totally avoids the subject of Eva, and he goes, am I like going out with anyone or anything, and I say no.

No, you said not right now, Ant interrupts me. Not right now, and then he goes: I bet you never did it. I bet you're still a virgin. And I thought that I would mess everything up if I told him that I had never done it, because then I was thinking about that slut Eva, and how if you ask me she like wasn't even a virgin when she was born, and I go: Yeah. Yeah, I've done it. Sure.

Too sly, goes Nunzi.

So tell her how he took it, goes Ant.

He took it real bad, and he totally swallowed the whole story right away. So he started to ask me who it was, and he started throwing out these names, and every time I said: I can't tell you. And he just kept hammering away.

Tell her about when he was pinching himself.

No, come on . . . Well, he was struggling to think of who it could be, and at the same time he kept pinching his thing. At least that's what it seemed like to me.

Get to the point, says Nunzi.

Come on, tell her about when he kissed you, Ant says again.

When he finally gets it through his head that Ant isn't coming, he stands up and he pulls me up too. He gloms onto me and squeezes me all tight and sticks like a foot-and-a-half of tongue into my mouth. So romantic.

Wow! goes Nunzi, with her eyes bugging out, he stuck his tongue in your mouth just like that? That is totally awesome, I'm serious. And what did you do?

I was like happy. I was thinking of the slut and I was all happy that I was groveling her boyfriend. And I was feeling totally good-looking, because Rino always has girlfriends who are so fine . . .

A little slutty, but fine, goes Ant.

And after the grovel?

Afterward, the dog went out and took a little walk with him, says Ant.

Do you mind if I tell it myself?

No! Don't tell me that you gave it up to Rino? I don't believe it.

Rossana Campo

He told her he only wanted to go somewhere where they could be alone for a little while. Can you believe that?

I thought that then maybe I could be his girlfriend.

Then you aren't too slick after all. He'll never leave Eva, that guy.

And then, she didn't even bleed, right?

But, are you sure you guys *really* did it? You went up to Costa?

Yeah. It was so hot . . .

But she started feeling funny about it. She says she got chicken.

If you ask me, you totally messed up, I'm telling you. That guy goes around and blabs everything.

That's what I told her, but she says she doesn't care. She is totally in love with the guy.

Nunzi is totally excited. She leans over to whisper in my ear, and she goes: What's it like? He seems like the kind of guy who has a really huge one.

It's like a banana, all curved over to the side.

Wow! goes Nunzi. Gino baby! Bring us three more, we have to celebrate. She pulls out a compact mirror and looks at her mouth and her eyes and smooths her tee shirt out over her tits, and then she goes: So you gonna see each other again?

Eva's coming back from the resort in September, goes Ant.

So then, what are you guys gonna do? I'm telling you, you better be careful 'cause that bitch doesn't play around. She'll slit your throat as soon as look at you. So watch out! Then she busts out laughing like a maniac.

He told her that they can't let Eva find out for a while. He said that once when she got jealous, she slashed the tires on his motorcycle, Ant informs her.

Gino brought the three beers, and Nunzi says: Let's toast! She gulps down half a glass of beer. Nobody around here is gonna tell your business, you can count on that. So you're not afraid of getting pregnant?

He says he was careful, says Ant.

And when the slut comes back, what the fuck are you gonna do? Nunzi asks again.

Heh, heh, goes Ant, what a nightmare! It's *too* messed up!

Anyway, we still have fifteen days, I go.

Fourteen, not counting today, Ant corrects me.

HAPPINESS

Maria Rosa Cutrufelli

"Shame? No. It is not out of shame that I've remained silent. Always. With everyone," said Lucia, turning away from the mountain and leaning back against the railing on the balcony. She couldn't bear the sight of the pinewoods that was gradually sliding down the eroding mountainside toward the town. Each summer she returned, and each summer a new ruin awaited her.

"A feeling of unease, perhaps. A retrospective discomfort that grew over the years. This, yes. Or, maybe, a regret." And she fell quiet. The story was lost in silence. Her friend raised her gaze patiently, inviting her to go on.

"I was nine years old. It's hard at that age to keep a secret. But I felt that I had to do it. There was something in our game that needed to be hidden. Even then I knew it. My body knew it, my hands, my fingers knew it, and that heat that rose, damp, ever so slowly, with a large and mysterious pulsing that did not come from the heart, was stronger than a heartbeat. I knew that it was a secret that needed to be hidden."

She turned back toward the mountain, forcing herself to look. The sunken road, badly eroded, that cut through the wood had almost disappeared, and was buried here and there under reddish dirt. It seemed as if a wave of subterranean force had thrust the trees upward, splitting the earth. The exposed roots dangled and waved, scrabbling at the crumbling raised edges of the roadway, vainly trying to grasp onto them as if fearful of all that freedom.

"Back then there was no asphalt, no road or cars. The pine-woods was intact. And right in front of it, right there, you see, where there are those cement houses with no stucco, that is where the gardens and orchards were."

Lucia remembered the oranges, tangerines, lemons, and the bulging, mature roses that opened their petals at the slightest breath, and the tart flavor of the stems of clover that made her squint.

"And those ruins down there were a house. Antonio's house."

It was an April day. Easter, with its marzipan lambs and chocolate eggs, had just passed. That morning, in class, the sun beat upon her neck and notebook. In the gardens that late afternoon, an almost summerlike silence descended.

"You could hear only the voices of my mother and my grandmother as they chatted while hoeing and pruning. Only their distracted voices in the background. A kind of sing-song, a familiar air that rose from the valley floor and accompanied me along the pathway. Up, up, into the pinewoods. It was my moment of freedom."

With a sharply pointed stick she turned over stones to surprise the snails underneath. Under every stone the earth was a different color, fresher and more brilliant. The snails shrank back into their shells, frightened by the sudden light. They

Maria Rosa Cutrufelli

became numb. Dead things. Except for that fine ring of slaver that, slightly frothing, revealed a vulnerability.

Then the pathway diverged. To the right it continued to rise and entered the pinewoods. To the left it began to descend again, toward the dump and the embankment on which ran the railroad tracks.

"That is where my walk would end."

It wasn't the pinewoods, then, that attracted her, but the underbrush, the charred trunks that smelled of smoke, the low hillside and the disorder of the garbage that hid wonderful surprises. A rolling can that reverberated. A bicycle chain. A book with pages that were torn but still legible. Nor did she like the smell of the forest, resinous, clean. The air there smelled like solitude. What she liked was the blast of wind made by a passing train, a hot smack, thick with promises, that took away one's breath.

"I used to wait for the five o'clock express. My hands covering my ears, my shoulders hunched to meet the impact head on. Then I would go back."

Along the banks of the tracks grew tall plants, brambles. No one was ever there. But Lucia had discovered a sign of human presence: the tops of some of the bushes had been tied together so as to create a protected cavity, the curved and transparent dome of a cupola. Someone came there to play, like she did.

Within that fragile shelter, before turning back the way she came, she stopped, while just above her, on the rocky and barren crest of the railway embankment, on the naked rails, the train cars rolled and flew on.

She lifted her dress, bent her knees, her buttocks resting on her heels, just slightly raised off the ground. She tried to get in position, bunching her short skirt against her belly, a skirt that was still full enough to form a complete wheel around Lucia when she felt the impulse to whirl around in place, sometimes, in a feat of dexterity, upon only one leg.

Her bladder was so full of urine that it hurt. A few drops

had already escaped, dampening her white cotton panties. She didn't take them completely off. She lowered them to just below her knees and then held them with both hands so as to not let them fall. She closed her eyes in pleasure at the sensation of the full, hissing current. A gush, and then a brief cessation to take a breath. Then another gush, and another breath. A third and final gush streamed with such force from her body that it sprayed the insides of her thighs, a slight, tepid tickle, a dusting of microscopic droplets. The ground underneath her voraciously absorbed one flow after another, but then restored it fizzing to the surface. A rivulet had already formed that ran off before disappearing. Some blades of grass dripped with moisture as if they had been rained upon. Lucia felt the tartness of clover between her teeth. It was a taste she would have liked to hang on to.

She squeezed her underwear harder in her left fist and, carefully, immersed the tip of her right index finger in the dwindling jet. She remained a moment like that, unmoving, as if waiting for something. Then, with a kind of sudden inspiration, slightly moving the white cotton clutched in her fist, she began to search for that little promontory, hairless and smooth like her cheeks. Hesitating, circumspect, she drew the tip of her finger, damp with urine, close to the fleshy border that opened onto an internal pulsing. The pulsing became a fevered pit-a-pat, an insistent thumping. The point of her finger, pure incandescence. She passed it once, twice, along the cleft, each time parting, probing with greater determination. The swollen flesh unclosed and captured that concentrated flame. She began to slide her finger with studied slowness up and down along the humid valley and the hills, elastic like sponge, that hid craters of fire, up and down gathering the last drops, up and down searching for the font of that shivering pleasure, that responsive point that she felt throb and throb.

It was the first time that she had explored herself so intently.

She closed her eyes again. She clamped them tightly so as to fully savor a tiny electric tremor, intense, almost painful.

Maria Rosa Cutrufelli

When she opened them the boy was right in front of her.

The surprise froze them both. He, bent slightly forward, a lock of light blond hair falling over his forehead, in the act of passing through the archway of the hut into what apparently was his secret place of play. Lucia was on her haunches, her legs beginning to give way from the awkward position and from the tension that had been accumulating, uncontrollably, explosively, under the gentle pressure of her forefinger.

"I found him extremely handsome. A big boy, not a kid like my schoolmates. I didn't know him. I had never seen him in town," she added, in a tone of defiance that her friend wasn't quite able to make out.

"I didn't know him. But I was not afraid when he slowly slid to the ground, almost kneeling, right in front of me."

They looked directly at each other, while the last echoes of the train dissipated into silence behind the mountain.

Lucia would have liked to close her legs, pull up her underwear, and run away. Away, quickly away, far from that sudden guilty feeling. Instead, she was unable to move or to halt the tremors that began at the tip of her finger and ran down her spine. She was no longer able to control the pulsing that from that miniscule nub of newly budding flesh, time and again sought for, caressed, touched, from that tiny point first lost then found, expanded outward like the rhythm of a train, multiplied like the echo of thunder. She felt a feverish ardor burning in her eyes.

In his eyes instead there was an innocent, shy curiosity, still distant from that of adulthood, and the singular, slightly melancholy sweetness of a puppy. He wore white sneakers and a light-colored shirt with short sleeves. His gaze wandered, amazed, inquisitive, from Lucia's face to her spread legs, to the long cleft that opened to reveal red clay between the saline white of her thighs, to the rivulet of urine that continued to wind among the clods of dirt at her feet. A gaze that excited her more than the touch of her by now knowing fingers, and it stirred that secret ember that had been hidden in her body and then so miraculously discovered. Lucia knew that she wanted, wanted desperately, for him to continue to watch her like this.

But the boy stretched out a hand—a hand more adult than his eyes. He pulled it back. Then he extended it again to catch upon his fingertip a drop of urine hanging from the taut elastic of her panties. He tested its consistency between thumb and forefinger, then raised his head toward her and laughed. It was a strange laugh, the laugh of a child who was both lost and greedily hungry. Lucia saw his teeth, so white, his large lips curled back, a wet strand of saliva upon them. She felt the muscles of her thighs tighten for a new exertion. His hand continued to move, ever so slowly retracing the damp track of the urine, which had taken on the color of dust. From time to time it stopped to play with the still soft and muddy earth, sketching small furrows, circles, obscure graffiti. Suddenly, he raised his fingers to his lips.

Lucia felt an acid clump dissolve in her mouth. And again, the taste of clover stems nipped between her teeth.

With the tip of his tongue, meanwhile, he tasted the mixture. He savored it, sucking slowly. He smelled his fingers, wet with saliva, searching for its odor. Then his hand would again begin its slow journey. It stopped ultimately when it reached a point just below that cleft, open and glistening with a moisture that was no longer urine.

And again, the boy searched her eyes, as if he had no idea what to do next.

The emotion of the moment created a sense of dizzying bewilderment in Lucia. The roar of the train had remained inside her and, entrapped, beat against her temples, rumbled in her vitals, could not escape. A new impatience impelled it now. That hand that barely grazed her, cautious, hesitant, that chafed her inflamed flesh a little with its slightly rough back side, that hand let loose a powerful heat in her; it melted her innards, possessed the force of attraction of a lodestone. Lucia

Maria Rosa Cutrufelli

touched it, grasped it, and taught the fingers of the boy that which hers had just learned.

It was only a day or two later that Lucia found out the boy's name. She found it out, as it happened, from her mother.

She was, as always, closing the shutters in the kitchen, like she always did in the evening before going to bed. Lucia saw her hesitate, her gaze directed toward someone or something.

"They're back," she said. "There's a light on in the first-floor apartment."

Lucia's grandmother shook her head and continued to work, picking out, with great precision, the little brown stones hiding among the dry lentils and piling them up on the table.

"They're kidding themselves," she remarked.

"Living in the city, with a boy like that . . . Here it's all much easier."

"They're kidding themselves," her grandmother replied, tossing the lentils into the pan. They clittered like hail on a windowpane. "The city is a bad place."

"But Antonio doesn't bother anyone. And here he is more free."

"Antonio is not like other people."

No, Antonio was not like other people. Antonio did not go to school. Antonio did not have friends. Antonio never spoke.

"I never found out what illness Antonio suffered from. He never spoke, but he was not mute. He never went to school, but he was intelligent. Or at least so he seemed to me, whenever I was able to enter into the light of his eyes."

A light that, once captured, released vortices of sparks in the blood.

"He is not like other people," said her grandmother again. It was a conclusive pronouncement. And she lowered her voice, watching Lucia out of the corner of her eye. The girl was playing with the little stones on the table, building and destroying five-pointed stars, flowers, filiform figures. Her head was lowered in an attitude of false concentration, of studied indifference.

"I'm not like other people, either," she thought proudly. "They" didn't know it, but her heart did not beat with the same rhythm as others'. It was a special heart belonging to a special little girl.

But Antonio's difference was greater. So great that it filled the room and the conversations of adults. And this, all of a sudden, hurt her. She felt a pang of envy, of jealousy. Then once again her admiration for him reasserted itself. There was a mystery about him that made him fascinating, terribly fascinating, more fascinating than any other boy. An enigma that captivated you, that you could not shake off.

Perhaps it was the way her mother and grandmother spoke about him, in low tones, with significant pauses. There was a conspiracy surrounding Antonio, an intrigue of adults, a hidden plot, a net with tight knots, always waiting there out of view, ready to ensnare him. In the voices of the adults there was something that she did not know how to interpret, a hard and unjust hostility that would never allow itself to be seduced by that blond hair and that was indifferent to that childish laugh, gleeful and astonished.

"A threat that was never explicit," Lucia specified, leaning toward her silent friend, almost as if she wanted to command her attention.

"And yet so clear, so impending. It was this threat that convinced me to keep our encounters secret."

The afternoons were long by the railway embankment, under the plaited bushes that formed the skeleton of a hut.

When Lucia arrived, he would never be there. She would push aside the brambles and enter underneath the branches, searching in vain for the white gleam of his shirt. In a daze, she would peer all around her, immersed in a strange sense of unreality, fearful and anxious at the thought of having lost him, of his having been swallowed up irretrievably by his own mystery and by the malice of adults. At the mere thought of it, her heart would tumble into a bottomless chasm and would be crushed, over and over again, under the wheels of a train with a thousand cars. And thus the customary acts would begin to be repeated, as if they were some rite of appeasement.

Her anxiety would be calmed the very moment at which she pulled down her panties and, squatting, sought the proper position, grasping her slightly spread knees. That was the signal. While she was crouched over to watch the hot urine running beneath her, he would suddenly appear, and would be watching her with that same inquisitive gaze as the first time, eager and attentive. It was as if she were the adult and he, the child.

Lucia knew that there was something in their game that left it terribly fragile. From one moment to the next, it all could cave in on them, within them. With the force of a train that derails. She had come to understand it, just like she had understood that it was important to repeat everything, exactly, in the very same order, following the same outline, everything just like the first time. Gestures, movements. Nothing could change. And as long as nothing changed, their game was safe. They were safe.

For a week or so, they didn't see each other. It rained and rained. There was no escape, no refuge, from that unseasonable rain, rude and exasperating. Everyone, adults and children, stayed in staring outside, fogging up the windowpanes, waiting futilely for some respite. School was out and the countryside was a sea of mud. One day when she attempted to go outside, her mother ran after her. She cuffed her soundly on the side of the head.

"Inside. Immediately."

The tears she fought back stung her eyes, tears for the injustice and powerlessness to which she was condemned by being a child.

She made an attempt to play by herself, mentally mixing the warmth of her fingers with the memory of the warm urine. The one called up the other in an automatic association, by now necessary, inevitable. Her flesh swelled, flowered, exploded at the combined sensation. Never, however, with the absolute intensity, the lightning spasm, that the gaze of Antonio caused in her. His gaze even more so than his hands—or rather, than the anticipation of his hands—or than the heat of his fingers.

As the days passed by one after another, a filthy cloud condensed around her, choking off her breath. In the stifling kitchen, already dark by early afternoon, her desire became something unctuous. It transformed into a turbid, sticky melancholy, a grimy anguish. Diseased.

Only Antonio's laugh could cure her. That hesitant laugh, disquieting like a difficult question that no one knew how to answer. No one save for the child Lucia.

She heard her mother talking about her: "She's becoming unbearable."

Finally, the sun returned, and the summer. The brambles along the pathway were already dusty, but in the dump the old newspapers rotted in a soggy heap. Only the hard cover of a book still held out. The title, stamped in faded gold, was just barely legible. *The Daughter of the Swamp King,* Lucia made out. But when she opened it, there was nothing inside, just some stray paper fibers still stuck to the spine.

She went on her way again. She forced herself to walk slowly, controlling her impatience by counting her footsteps, nine, ten, and then beginning all over again. But in the final stretch of road she could hold out no longer, and she ran and ran until she was out of breath.

Antonio was standing straight upright in the middle of the bushes, now leafless because of the rains. His eyes glanced around uneasily, his hands restlessly tracing gestures, words

Maria Rosa Cutrufelli

in the air. It was as if he were asking someone to account to him for all that disaster. Lucia stopped to catch her breath. For the first time, he had arrived there before she did. She looked at him, still as if from a great distance, and he seemed to her taller and thinner, more handsome. But also more mysterious, enclosed as he was within his frail carapace, a snail shell that one could easily crush between two fingers. A few weeks had been time enough to change him. She drew near him with a hesitancy that made her legs tremble.

And then he finally focused his gaze on her. Lucia continued to advance, ever closer. She saw him nervously shifting his weight, as if he were readying himself to flee. Then, little by little, his face lost that suffering, dark expression. His hands descended, relaxed, to his sides. Lucia got closer still, holding her breath, her heart beating crazily. She slowly drew her body to his. And it was the first time. She felt him trembling against her, upon his shirt she could smell the pungent odor of cat fur and wet earth. She raised her face to look him in the eyes. And he laughed his happiness down upon her. His breath was nice, slightly tart.

Lucia raised herself up on tiptoe and pressed her lips against his. She opened them and passed the tip of her tongue along the interlocked outer surface of his teeth. His tongue responded with a gritty, furtive touch.

That strong and mysterious pulsing began again in Lucia's body. She grabbed his hand and guided it under her skirt, inside her panties. She opened her thighs while the urine cascaded on her impatient fingers, down her thighs and then down over her calves to her ankles; it soaked her woven sandals and Antonio's tennis shoes. It was tepid, and then suddenly cold, tepid then cold, and then only cold, a marvelous cold stream that burned.

Her right hand, guiding, was forcing his hand. With the other, in the meantime, she blindly searched for the fly of his jeans. She didn't even know herself, actually, what she was trying to discover and why. She could do nothing but pursue her desire, one that, while confused, was nonetheless quite precise. She wanted him to reveal himself before her, wanted his hot jet on her fingers, wanted to see and to feel, to enter into his stream, first tepid, then cold, then hot again, then fresh like a mountain stream to which one comes to slake one's thirst.

Instead, he hardened.

But Lucia could no longer stop herself. A pressing urgency was burning in her that demanded that she hold him prisoner, that she squeeze him tightly against her. But it was a tender imprisonment, one that did not disguise its snares.

With her tongue she wet his lips again, almost as if to reassure him, while she slowly continued to open his jeans, slowly caressed, touched, extracted his sex from its damp dwelling in his undershorts. It swelled rapidly, naked and red, in her hand. She felt it palpitate while a clear jet, thicker than urine, spurted onto her wrist.

Lucia got frightened. She opened her fingers, loosening her grip. There was a stickiness on her palm, and the exposed flesh lying there trembled.

"I'm sorry," she said, breaking the silence. "I'm sorry. I hurt you." And they were the first words to ever pass between them. But when she looked at him again, raising her eyes, he had a smile on his face, vacant and happy. Then, suddenly, he stretched out his arms, with a jerk of his head flipped the blond lock of hair behind him, and let out a long, hoarse sigh to the heavens. Then, just like that, with his jeans open and his sex still dripping, he took off, running down along the embankment, leaping, laughing, waving his hands in the air as if in a greeting of insane, irrepressible happiness.

"I never saw him again. Never, ever again. I waited for him in vain, entire days, the trains kept passing one after another up there on the embankment. But Antonio never came. I cried, believing I had wounded him, fatally perhaps. And the memory of his shout of joy, of the astounding mania of happiness that overcame him, gave me no consolation. I cried for my impatience, for that heedless desire that had erased him like

Maria Rosa Cutrufelli

that, pitilessly, from my daytimes, now so miserably interminable without him. I hadn't respected the rules of our game, and this was my punishment. But why did desire have to have so high a price?"

Lucia sighed, staring at the pinewoods. The shadows were descending to blanket it, rapidly, progressively, inevitably. The sun was already behind the mountain, and with it a distant rumbling of trains.

"Then I realized that in his absence something strange was hidden. As if that mystery that I had become aware of in the comments of the adults, in that far-off gaze of his, in that questioning laugh, had suddenly materialized, somewhere. Perhaps this was why my mother and grandmother no longer spoke about him. No one spoke about him. Antonio had disappeared, for everyone. But not for my body, not for my heart. My heart wanted to know, demanded an explanation."

She gathered up all her courage. She defeated her reluctance. "Where is Antonio?" she asked her mother one day.

The woman shut off the faucet and turned to look at her, wiping her hands on her apron. In her eyes shone an unsavory suspiciousness, a malevolent light.

"What do you know about Antonio?" And again: "What do you know?"

"Nothing," Lucia quickly replied, frightened by the change in her mother's voice, in her expression. "Nothing. You and Grandma . . . you always talked about him. I heard you."

"Oh, is that it? Now you try to eavesdrop on the conversations of grown-ups."

The little girl swallowed hard, trying not to cry. "No, no, I don't eavesdrop on you. And I don't know anything. Nothing!" she screamed, and fled into the courtyard. She wept for a long time, uncontrollably, her face pressed against a wall. "Nothing," she stammered through her sobs, "I don't know anything."

"And that," said Lucia finally, "that was the ultimate betrayal."

THE RED BATHROBE

Erminia Dell'Oro

It seemed like I was being slowly extinguished in the anonymous, gray city where I had come to pursue my studies. I thought about the light I had left behind in my hometown, about my house, about my friends.

In the morning, while I was opening the shutters, the gray of the sky would enter into my soul. It was always an effort to start the day, to take the bus, to go to the university. I observed everything around me as if it were not I living my life, but another, or my double, lost in an immense solitude.

I had just taken a shower one morning when the doorbell rang. I went to the intercom.

"I'm a representative of Mondia Publishers. I'm sure you've heard of it. We also put out encyclopedias. I saw you yesterday in the bookstore talking to Mrs. Donno. She was the one who gave me your address. I have a proposition to make to you which I think you will find interesting."

I thought about the books I had left in Cairo. I only had a

few now, some of the classics in cheap editions that I had been buying in Luciana's bookstore.

"I'm in a hurry," I replied, "I have to go to the university, I'm late."

"I'll only need a minute. I'll come up and leave you some catalogs. Then you can call me to set up an appointment."

It was a beautiful voice, young and intense.

"Who knows how many books," I thought, "could be in those catalogs."

I thought also that I could not receive an unknown visitor wearing only my bathrobe, but I didn't have enough time to dress. I wrapped the robe tightly around me and cinched the tie. I wouldn't let him in. The man only had to give me the catalogs, then he would leave. I opened the door.

Out of the elevator came a man of about forty years old, tall, thin, with a black raincoat on.

"Excuse me," I said, showing only my face, "I must get dressed. If you like, you can just leave me the catalogs, and I . . . "

"Don't worry," he interrupted me, and pushed open the door.

"You're dressed. You look good in red."

He came into the vestibule.

"I'm late," I said, in a voice that came out quite different. I was shocked. I found myself in an absurd situation. Standing in front of me, in my own house, an unknown man, one who had entered against my will, was observing me. I had nothing on but a bathrobe, and I was doing nothing to get rid of him.

It seemed as if I was paralyzed, as if all my bodily energies, as well as my voice, had abandoned me. My hands, which were clenching the knot tying my bathrobe closed, were sweaty.

He stared at me, in no way bothered by my obvious discomfort.

"May I see your library?" he asked me after a moment. His tone of voice was calm and polite.

"Would you please leave?" I managed to say.

Erminia Dell'Oro

"Really?" He smiled pleasantly. I thought that he must be joking—that it was a bad joke—or that he wanted to provoke me. He walked into my apartment's only room, a living room with a sofa bed. He looked at the books on my shelves, picked one up, and flipped through the pages. I was incapable of insulting him, though I wished I could, for that unjustifiable behavior.

"Mrs. Donno spoke to me of you," he said, his finger resting on the first page of the book he had in his hand. "You've come from Egypt?"

His face, mutable, conveyed restlessness, curiosity.

"Yes," I replied, trying to calm myself down. "My father is a diplomat. We often change cities, continents."

My heart was pounding. I wanted to make him understand that I was a respectable girl, not used to hosting men at her home, and especially not dressed this way.

"Now," I begged him, "can you leave?"

He approached me. He untied the knot of my bathrobe and removed it, letting it fall to the ground. I smelled tobacco and cologne on him, felt his hands, warm, on my body. He kissed my neck, behind my ears, he caressed my pelvis.

I would have wanted to cry, to scream, out of humiliation for my weakness, but I was unable to repulse him. I had never before felt those spasms shooting through my body, those sensations of desire and pleasure exploding in my head.

"Until tomorrow," he said after a few moments. "I will come tomorrow evening." I caught up the bathrobe and quickly put it on. I was out of breath.

"Not tomorrow evening," I managed to say. "The woman who rented me this apartment lives across the hall. During the day she is not home, but in the evening she is. I can't have . . . men here."

"Fine," he said, "I will come tomorrow morning. At nine. Wear the bathrobe again." He stroked my face. He had a disarming smile; he seemed, in that moment, very young.

Thus began my affair with Paolo. My relationship with that man was always ambiguous. I didn't care to know who he was, how he lived, or to make plans for the future. But I was tormented by my desire for him, and by the sensations that I felt, completely new to me, which caused me to feel extreme guilt. I could no longer concentrate on my studies. I stopped seeing those few friends from the university who had been trying to help me find my feet there.

Paolo was strange, sometimes taciturn, sometimes talkative, and he never spoke at all about himself. Gradually, he became more and more possessive, and more violent when we were making love.

He came up to my apartment in the morning, then later would give me a ride to the university, and return to pick me up. In the evening we would eat dinner in a little trattoria near the canals. Then we would make love in the car. Every day, while I was wearing the bathrobe as I waited for him to arrive, I would realize that I did not love him as I would have liked. But the inexhaustible, sometimes painful, desire for the pleasure that he gave me took away my ability to reason with the necessary lucidity.

I began to be unable to endure his company. I suspected that he was no longer going to work. He was shabby, obsessive, jealous. I would have liked to lock myself away in my single room forever.

My sexual desire for him also waned. I could think of him without feeling those twinges in my groin, those tremors running through me, as in the first months.

I was no longer able to bear his violence. In the moments in which he held me with my face pressed against the mattress, I felt like I was suffocating, and I struggled to free myself, screaming.

Paolo had become an obstacle that I did not know how to avoid.

It was then, when he realized that my feelings for him were changing, that he mentioned marriage.

"We will get married," he said, "we will get married soon."

Erminia Dell'Oro

Alarmed, I changed the subject. I didn't even know who he was, that man!

One evening, my landlady stopped me outside of the front door. "I don't want to interfere in your affairs," she said in a kindly tone, "but your mother has been begging me to. So many awful things happen in the world. That man who is always here is your fiancé? I heard that he has been asking the doorkeeper questions. He seems so jealous, I wouldn't want . . . and he is also much older than you are."

"The doorkeeper should mind her own business, don't you think?" I curtly replied. "However, he is a friend of mine. But I will only be seeing him for a short while longer."

The next day I received a letter from my mother. I had spoken to her on the phone a few days previously, and she seemed worried.

"A certain Paolo S.," my mother wrote, "has informed your father by letter that he would like to marry you. Why didn't you let us know anything about this? And this is a relationship that has been going on for months now. I've called your land-lady. We don't want to check up on you, my dear, but you're twenty years old. You live alone in a strange city. You are constantly seen in the presence of a man much older than you. We know nothing about it, and then a request for your hand in marriage arrives, even a request for your birth certificate to apply for a marriage license. Your father wants me to come immediately to Italy, but I think of you, even still, as a sensible girl, just like you've always been. You come here. We'll expect you at your next break. Leave early."

I felt the desire to rebuke Paolo the next time I saw him, but I could not bring myself to do it. He seemed more frazzled, more worried than usual. I was afraid of how he might react, and of the look in his eyes, which seemed sometimes like that of a madman.

I calmed myself down by thinking that only a short time remained before the Christmas holidays, a month and a half, and that I would leave early. I would not mention it to Paolo.

I was tormented by conflicting feelings for Paolo: I found

him increasingly intolerable, but I felt pity at seeing him so broken-down, and I was apprehensive. I observed him and wondered all the while who he was, actually, that stranger. But, as if by tacit agreement, I continued not to ask questions. Furthermore, I no longer really even cared. One evening, in a trattoria, there was a heated discussion between us. Paolo spoke to me of our marriage, which he took for granted, of the paperwork still to be done, and of a house, wherever that might be.

"I don't want to marry you," I said, after having tried to change the subject. I stood up and headed toward the door. Paolo followed me, he insulted me in the middle of the street. He pushed me into the car and forcefully tore my pants off.

That night my mother called me. "Another letter arrived," she said, trying to maintain an even tone of voice. But I could immediately tell that she was disturbed. "It was addressed to me this time, and I will not show it to your father. That man is insane. I don't know what is happening to you, but you no longer seem like our little girl, like this . . ."

I began to scream at her. I had been living in a state of extreme tension for months, and I could not just sit there and listen to the criticisms of my mother, the litany of unhappiness and disappointments that I was causing her, now that I was no longer "their little girl, like this . . ."

"You don't understand anything! It's easy for you to . . . lecture me," I shouted.

"Well then listen," she brusquely interrupted me. "I will read you the first lines of that gentleman's letter: 'As I have already written, I would like to marry your daughter as soon as possible. She is the kind of girl that used to be called *easy,* and she needs someone by her side. Do you know how she received me the first time? She had never seen me before; I was coming up to leave her some catalogs. She was wearing a red robe, open. She is striking when dressed—imagine how she looks naked. It is no wonder that we wound up in bed. I could not restrain myself, but I know that with me she will be happy.'"

Erminia Dell'Oro

I slammed down the phone. My mother was a fascinating woman, modern, relatively independent-minded, considering the environment in which she lived and the temperament of my father, a man very bound to tradition. She was the one who had encouraged me to move to Italy to study archaeology.

I wept tears of anger, of humiliation. In that moment I wished my mother would disappear, so as to erase, with her, the words she had said, which burned unbearably inside me. I hated Paolo. Only a madman could behave that way. There was no justification for him to have written a letter that would have had such dramatic consequences for me if my father had read it.

I fell asleep, exhausted, with the light on.

I dreamed of being by the sea, on the shore of a white, deserted beach. I let myself enter the water. The waves penetrated my vagina; I shivered all over and felt intense pleasure pervading me. I would have liked to drift far away, into the sea, into the light.

I was in a deep sleep when Paolo entered the apartment, shortly before dawn. He took off my nightgown. He caressed me, delicately. I was dreaming of the waves entering inside of me, the water, warm, between my legs. Slowly coming back to consciousness, I felt him on top of me, and the desire for the sea, the pleasure I had felt in my sleep, melded into desire for him.

"Turn over, my love," he murmured in my ear, "turn over." On my knees, I held on to the headboard of the bed, still lost between sleep and waking. He gripped my shoulders so tightly that it hurt. The vision of the sea, of the waves, was lost in the distance. There was only him, inside my body, and the spasms that shot through me.

"That's enough now, Paolo," I said later while we were having coffee. "I want my house keys back. Leave me in peace. I need tranquility. I have to study, and I'm no longer able to get anything done."

I didn't speak to him about the letter. I tried to stay calm. I was afraid of his insanity.

He did not respond. He was pale, unkempt. He no longer paid attention to anything except me. I wondered how he could continue to go on in that way.

One morning, when we were getting out of bed, I received a call from an airline company agent. They had a prepaid ticket, in my name, destination Cairo, Saturday night departure.

I lied to Paolo, ever suspicious, telling him that the university had called to confirm an exam date.

The following morning he didn't come up to the apartment. He waited for me outside.

"I'll make you a proposition," he said, "my last one. I've thought a lot about us. There is no solution to our situation but to leave each other. I want to change my life. I have some interesting plans. I'm moving, I'm changing everything." He smiled. I watched him, trying to understand. Paolo's smile, pleasant, affectionate, which made him appear much younger than he was, amazed me every time, stirring in me a feeling of profound melancholy. I would have liked to erase every trace of that relationship.

"I would like to talk to you," he added, "but not here. Let's go to the lake, we can come back this evening. I want to show you the house where I spent my childhood years."

"The lake?" I was dismayed. I had no fondness for lakes. They seemed somber, still; they conveyed presages of death. I didn't want to see Paolo's house, nor hear him speak of his childhood, now that I was about to leave him.

"The lake?" I repeated, trying to gain some time.

"Please. It is the last time that we will see each other, I promise. I need to spend an hour or two with you at the lake." He was speaking in deep, persuading tones that affected me. "I loved that house very much, but I will sell it. I'm changing my life, I told you."

I felt that Paolo was not lying to me, that maybe he would find a sense of well-being and purpose again.

"I have an important class today." I tried, again, to ward off his proposition.

"Oh please, dear."

There was light, the light of an autumn day, which to me seemed suffused with separations, farewells.

"It's a beautiful day," said Paolo, looking up at the sky. "It won't be cold at the lake."

"Let's come back early, then, in the afternoon."

"I promise."

The shoreline of the lake was mottled with gold, copper, dusky green. The water was immobile. I got out of the car, ran to the edge, and looked down, trying to see something lying on the bottom. There were only shadows. I thought of the sea, mutable, alive, the sea that I loved so much.

There were no boats on the lake. A seagull skimmed over the surface. The house was large. It had peeling walls and an overgrown garden with persimmon trees growing in it. The fruit seemed to catch fire in the light of the sun on the already bare branches.

The rooms smelled musty. Paolo opened the kitchen shutters. There was an old blackened stove, and copper pans hung everywhere.

"I'm cold," I said. I hugged myself in my heavy jacket. It felt like a weight was pressing down upon my chest. I wanted to flee, return immediately home.

Paolo lit the stove, then he went to close the door. I heard the key turn several times in the lock, and the sound of the door chain.

"Now let's talk," he said, coming back in and taking me by the hand. He brought me into the adjoining room, a living room with sofas and armchairs with faded slipcovers. The walls were hung with pictures of stern-faced women and views of the lake. Paolo, seated next to me on the sofa, spoke without ceasing even for a moment. I remained silent. I was anxiety-stricken. I had visions of the airplane that would carry me home.

"Paolo," I said finally. "You said that we were leaving each other. Are you having second thoughts? You promised me . . ."

He rose and went into the room next door. He returned with a red robe and a pair of scissors.

"What are you doing?" I asked him. My heart was beating hard.

"Take down your hair."

I hesitated, then I decided to obey him. I was afraid. I took off my hair clip. My hair cascaded upon my shoulders, down my back.

"Take off your clothes, dear." Paolo was smiling.

I wrapped my arms around my body.

"Take off your clothes," he repeated.

I took off my jacket, my sweater, my shirt, I slipped out of my pants.

"Take off all your clothes."

Trembling, I unhooked my bra, took off my panties.

"Now," he said, stroking my face, "I'm going to cut off your hair."

I was cold, afraid. He had me put on the robe, then he began to cut my hair. The long locks fell to the ground, dark blotches upon the yellowed floor.

I passed a hand over my head. My hair was short, like a boy's. I remembered that when I was a little girl, my mother used to take me often to the hairdresser's to have my hair cut, very short. She had so much wanted a boy, they used to tell me, before I was born. Perhaps it was the disappointment at having had a girl that led her to dress me for years in boy's clothes. As I got older I rebelled. I continued to wear pants, as one normally did by that time, but my hair had grown very long.

"You look nice," Paolo murmured. He stroked my legs. "You look like a boy, so thin, with you hair cut short."

He pulled the slipcover off one of the armchairs. The cushions were of blue velvet.

"Sit down, dear."

I let myself onto the armchair. I rested my head against its back and stretched out my legs.

Erminia Dell'Oro

I had been, in a certain sense, kidnapped, but I had allowed Paolo to cut my hair, without resisting, and not only out of fear.

I was doing everything that he asked me to, no longer afraid. I had totally given myself over to his desire.

He, standing in front of me, looked down at me. But I had a feeling, during those moments, that his thoughts were elsewhere.

Then he stretched out his hands to mine and lifted me up. I followed him as he made his way into another room. My temples pulsed with a quickening rhythm, and tiny tremors ran through my body.

He pulled me to him in the cold bed.

"You seem like a boy, with your hair short." He spoke in his beautiful deep voice in my ear.

I took his hands, guided them to my pelvis, my breast, my throat.

"Squeeze," I said, "why don't you kill me?"

I rocked in our fatal game, stimulated by pleasure and torment. I felt my head shatter, my body explode.

"Turn over."

I obeyed, letting him be the one to determine the rules.

On my knees, I grasped the headboard.

Outside it was dark. The trees had vanished, the persimmons, the far-off hills. In the room, the oppressive furniture, the blotches of mold, all was vanishing. A bird cried out in the night.

I moaned, calling out to him, inside of me, desiring him to love me, beyond every imaginable possibility.

Suddenly, I rebelled. Turning over with a jerk, I pushed him away with my arms, my legs.

"Leave me alone!" I shouted, "leave me."

Paolo turned on the lamp on the nightstand. He was smiling, looking at me. He held me still, by force. He gripped my skin between his fingers, making me scream in pain.

We fell asleep at daybreak.

I woke up late. Blades of cold light entered through the shuttered windows. I was momentarily disoriented. I didn't know where I was. Then I remembered. Paolo was gone. The red robe was on the floor at the foot of the bed.

I got up, ran into the living room to get my clothes, and dressed hurriedly. I could think of nothing but fleeing. I threw open the shutters, climbed out the window, and ran to the gate. It was open.

I ran along the pathway without looking back, out of fear of seeing him. I started at every rustle. There were no houses around, no one was there. On the motionless water a seagull floated.

I reached a gas station. A young woman gave me a ride to a train station in a nearby town. I didn't go home. I called a friend of mine from the university and asked if I could stay with her.

I was able to depart for Cairo the following night, as I had planned.

I returned to Italy three months later and went to pick up my belongings in the apartment I was leaving. The doorkeeper told me that Paolo had not been seen again.

Twelve years passed. I had achieved my childhood dream: I became a good archaeologist. I lived in Italy, but I spent long periods working abroad. I had also gotten married, to one of my teachers from the university, but the marriage only lasted three years. He could not endure my frequent absences or my desire for independence. One evening, I returned to the book-store that I had patronized during my first year of university. I had never returned to Luciana's bookstore for fear of meeting Paolo.

The bookseller remembered me. I worked our conversation around to Paolo.

I had expelled any thought of him for years. But suddenly a desire arose in me to know what had become of that strange person from that relationship that had seemed unreal, as if it had all been a story, another life, a dream.

"He disappeared," the bookseller said. "He simply abandoned his job one day, with unpleasant consequences for us. Someone told me—but it was only a rumor—that he had become a vagabond, or something like that; others took him for dead. He was very capable at his job, polite, even charming sometimes, but truly strange. I wouldn't be surprised to see him walking around one day like a street person. Back then, when he used to come here, I didn't know his story. Then I found out."

"His story?" I was tense, hoping that no one would come in and interrupt her narrative. They called her to the phone, then she had to attend to a customer for some time. She returned. She seemed eager at the prospect of relating something interesting.

"The woman he lived with for a year or so," she proceeded, "spoke to me of him. I believe she was in love with him, and she endured quite a bit as a result. Paolo had been left an orphan at the age of five. A terrible story, during the years of the Resistance. His father was a paralytic, but very active in politics, supported by his wife, a sociologist involved in various fields. They lived with the little boy and his sisters in a house on Lake Maggiore. Those were hard times, I lived through them, too. One evening a band of thugs entered their house. I don't know what they were looking for. They took the father and threw him in his wheelchair in the lake. Then they threw the mother, who had tried to defend him, in too.

"The child grew up with his aunts, who loved him very much. As a boy he studied with great success in Milan, physics perhaps, I don't remember. Then there was some kind of scandal, on account of which his aunts preferred that he no longer return to the lake.

"Paolo had fallen for the son of a rich landowner, a nobleman who had a villa on the outskirts of the city. He was a handsome boy, spoiled, about whom there was obviously a certain ambiguity.

"The boy was sent to study in the United States. I don't know how Paolo spent those years. Years later, I met the woman who had helped him and with whom he had lived. She too has not heard from him again."

Another telephone call interrupted the story. I paged through some books on the tables without even seeing them.

"Paolo painted," continued the bookseller, returning. "During the time of that boy. In his house, completely abandoned, on the lake were found some of his paintings. That woman took them. He had painted a portrait of the boy that was really very beautiful."

"And the woman?" I asked, after a moment of silence. "Do you still see her?"

"No, I haven't seen her for awhile. She had come asking me to help her sell the paintings. In the past we had been involved in art; we used to hold exhibitions. It was on that occasion that she told me the story of Paolo. He left her in extremely bad financial shape. He had asked her to lend him some money, and he had never returned it. I very much liked the painting of the boy. It had extremely vivid colors, very beautiful, the red of the robe that he was wearing, the blue of the cushions. I regret not having bought it myself, but it made me somehow uneasy. Maybe because I knew the story, I don't know. What a shame. He had talent . . ."

I thought back upon the faraway night on the lake. For the first time, after so many years, the events of that night, the hours passed in the cold rooms, reappeared in my memory with great clarity. I thought about the turmoil that had overtaken my life, about the silences of Paolo, about the woman who had lived with him.

I bought a book and left the bookstore.

It was a beautiful day. I felt like walking for a long time. I looked up at the limpid sky. I felt, upon my face, the pleasant warmth of spring in the cheerful city.

Erminia Dell'Oro

E N V Y

Marc de' Pasquali

My name is of no importance. They often call me Müsy. It is late morning, the beginning of another summer. Waiting for the ship that will take me back (maybe) to Turkey, attracted by an unusual sweet-briar bush, I am careful where I step— Venice is hot, dank, and besieged by cholera, while everything, even the circling of the seagulls, is chasing noontime.

In front of the Giudecca, I permit myself a brief pause in my brisk walk. My eyes are swollen, glazed over with absinthe, heavy with sleepiness; I sit down at a round, wobbly wrought iron table outside, notwithstanding the humidity. I am shivering; I order coffee.

"I want it Turkish style, with a little sugar."

Relaxed by the obedient manners of the waiter, I stretch my legs, slip off my gloves, lean my cane against the chair. I seat myself facing a pewter sun, and automatically begin to muse over whom I killed first this past night. The blasted Polish woman, of course. Sophie, last.

How could I not have done it? I was forced to, blackmailed in a deadly ploy. An execution. Brutal, like that of the ancient mariner who killed the albatross (I had browsed through the story in a gift book included with my *Corriere della sera*), a mutiny against faith, against the august harmony of nature, to be expiated—as if we didn't do that enough, shackled and slithering on this infinitesimal planet, that from one moment to the next can explode into nothingness.

I will have to retire, reflect, write it all out—as if that were easy in this 1891, year of the foundation of the National Literary Society.

What does any of the rest of it matter? I ramble on. The fervor of malaise is insatiable.

The century is coming to an end. Some are talking of war, between the resignation of Bismarck-Schönhausen, the republic in Brazil, the Portuguese expansion in Black Africa making the English begin to snarl. To conquer is to survive, always a matter of force. I can take it no longer. I would enter a monastery in a minute! I knew some harm would befall me returning to Venice. I am so completely exhausted, beaten. I want to disappear, if, that is, I've even been present in all this mindlessness, this theatricality, which I have a perfectly clear view of now, can finally see without regressing too much.

I met Sophie at the opera.

She had eyes like two green leaves announcing the tawny rays of autumn. She was Sinan's lover. Everyone knew it. Even though she had been with a woman, she was still incredibly alluring.

Two weeks thereafter she became mine, one fragrant dawn on the Golden Horn, where I live. I will never forget how my legs gave way under the savored orgasms; the two thousand strokes balanced upon one knee; the turgescent tongue that could no longer eat, speak, drink, laugh; her earlobes like cyclamens, her pupils dilated. And she, dear God, sweaty, with tiny nibbles murmuring come, come. And I, pressing ever closer upon her, overawed by the extreme comeliness of her hands that held me entirely in their palms, that excited me to salivation and to fantasy in the succession of bright dawns inflected by the cries of cocks. Ah, those fingers of unspeakable witchcraft, visible to the eye, which I longed to have upon me, in me, in my ass, in my heart—even in public!

We did nothing but dissipate up, up, at great length. Descent was impossible. We had time—celebrations only annul it.

Now, however, in her room, out of my wits in a drunken stupor, I violated that most delicious hand of cards, the rules of the game, by poisoning her; oh yes, I stuck her still and cold into a pile of rotting rose petals. Incredible.

How could I not have done it? True, to exterminate is the most banal of solutions. It is what damns and humiliates me, not fear. However, her constant presence exasperated me, as did her distance from me, and that unpredictable enthusiasm for the vast and the beautiful. What a struggle, between her elegance and my inability! She was, moreover, more elevated. And that way of hers, easy, trusting, grateful, almost angelic, struck one wherever she went, leaving you at one with the world. One felt (damn if it wasn't exhilarating!) that her poetic tension occupied only one day at a time, neither forbearance nor transport, illusions nor disappointments. Intolerable. Especially for me, harried as I am by my hopelessness, my incapacity for resilience, for transformation, all plainly evident in this watchful city, so cramped, treacherous, where even the stenches, the four hundred windows opening onto a single square, the cloistered spaces, the indifference to ruin, hound you.

One evening while climbing into an unsteady gondola, while the admiring gondolier was holding her arm, I caught a glimpse of her more smiling than usual. Envy.

I fell into a hateful, tyrannous mania.

I revenged myself by seizing the opportunity to woo a Polish woman, entirely yellow, masculine, false—a stepmother, several years older than I, garishly opulent (and large-veined), who astonished me with her pragmatic way of ingesting food while wheedling and flattering me. The thing was done.

Nothing was ever again the same. Embraces, jealousies, dangerous indecisions, packed bags.

Sophie and I separated decorously, with no farewell ceremonies.

On my way out of Europe, I paid a last visit to the Polish woman, who indifferently declared, one day you will return, our past is our future, Venice is irresistible, like God, to forget is impossible.

Damned if that prophetess molded in the orgies of Ephesus or writhing in the Parisian *affiches* of the noble Toulouse-Lautrec ever brooded over truth!

I am incapable of relating that winter passed in Istanbul: social calls, readings, garrulous adventures that could not ultimately seduce me, seize my mood, flow, engage my intelligence, which insanely licked, palpated, enjoyed, despaired.

During a spring ramble with some friends by the enchanted firesides of the Göreme Valley, under the roofs of dwellings flagellated by the most ancient ages of the world, sated by contemplation wine opium, I entreated a young man accompanying our travels and tending to our needs (as skilled as Sophie was in ministering to one even worn by fatigue) to permit me to try to handle and suck and squeeze—then in and out of the hole—his nauseating worm. Then with another, and yet again another. At times with satisfaction.

Their touch I would define as knowing; it was instinctive and impatient. It revealed such panicked longings in me that I would explode right from the preliminaries.

To receive blows upon the buttocks under the powerful smacking of the testicles (however spherical, compact, in no way pendulous or hairy, perfectly proportioned to the shaft); to follow alien, conclusionary rhythms; to suffer voluptuous, diffuse and lascivious egoisms normally reserved for the mildest feminine hearts; however all this might be, it is instructive. Certainly inconceivable to the unworldly.

And what I wished to prove or experience, other than the relation between events not comprehensible at first glance, I frankly wouldn't know, if not remote practices, struggle, suffering. Perhaps to share the sensation of that slithering thing that, if it entered the sainted belly of Sophie for love, entered me (with the help of some oil of bitter almond) out of hunger. Perhaps to simulate initial grand desires so as to receive the ecstasy of small parental affections.

I was, that is to say, confused.

At my wit's end, I sent her a brief letter by courier. Why this separation, this silence? We wanted to grow old together—my abundance, my Sophie, my faith my genius my fever bestowed upon life.

She replied. I embarked.

There was hot weather in Italy. Some boys were bathing in the canal just like in the painting by one of the nine sons of Tiepolo. Months and months had passed, but not the pain, nor the putrid resentment, and as soon as I docked I was struck by it.

Before going to Sophie's house, some force of inevitability carried me to the address of the Polish woman. Who, as ill-proportioned and invasive as ever, and by no means surprised, was taking a bath. She touched her breasts, barely, seductively, without seeming to do so and without hurry, and, on occasion, as her fingertips happened across them, her nipples: a business that one would have to have seen in order to fully appreciate the trembling of those vast dugs of hers, which did not even fail to emit a milky spritz. After a glass of marsala I embraced her, and was recompensed as only an attentive goddess—decisive, ready, large—is able to. I wet myself completely.

Entering into her rooms, between her legs, had extirpated a baffling sense of being adrift. The Polish woman excited me.

There was nothing for it. Yes, I had gone back to Venice. And I had gone backward. And the real reality of it all came home to me. Peevish, I got drunk.

I had no desire to see Sophie again. I no longer loved her. I no longer wanted her, but I was unable to be apart from her (however I might have believed, for some few instants, that I was). The wasted energy . . . I had always waited for her! She was the soul of my existence, of my creativity, of my phallus, lady and queen of my mystic nuptials—and it was over. Nothing would be, nothing was, different. I felt it. Having exhausted the initial emotion, the torment of her presence would drive me insane after minutes—slow ones.

What can it mean to give oneself over to the dream of the ideal woman, to meet her, recognize her, unveil her, after which, and ever so quietly, in the transitoriness sparked by separation, to deface her image and masturbate? Can it be that one, that I—unbridled wretch—though loathe to admit it, am a misanthrope? Is it possible, had I been more routinely unhappy, that deep within I would still have been the kind of man who supposed he had been granted to live several different lives?

The kind of man who squandered, who had not taken and not been taken, had not hearkened to colors, had only espied the stench of hate? Was my body truly unable to bear the idea of decaying near Sophie? Did I truly not want the same clean and meticulous old woman snoring beside me; not want the same slightly deaf conversations; the thoughts circulating in the void of stale armpits; the ideas paralyzed within an unfamiliar and timorous laziness; and onward! with the little slovenlinesses, hidden within the coils of the black reptile of habit, which would increase day by day, in regret and in praise, with the acid breath, the shirt more threadbare, the little rolled balls of bread on the tablecloth? Was it truly only an exotic blonde, a stereotype of the highest order, who would never enter her dotage with me, that I found attractive? To be sure!

I came and came, spraying everywhere, as much as the ma-

Marc de' Pasquali

ternal whey that issued from that big Polish beast, and joyfully, after having futilely sucked my wit dry for an entire year. A man is ever a man—and birds of a feather . . . Puerile!

A blaze was necessary. On account of my anguish, my rage, my cock charged with hysterical well-being.

"I disdain myself!" I howled, brandishing a flaming candlestick.

Fire.

Then curtains paper screens dressing gowns embroidered veils satin pillows kilim peacock feathers leather-bound volumes chinoiserie and other frippery, all gone.

The Polish woman, chaotically stitched over with my dangling droplets discharged moments before into her navel, reacted impulsively to the heat of the flames that licked at her skin, and like a swollen goose in peignoir, attempting to grasp onto me, gave me a swat that made the head of my cock bounce and gyrate, then convulse in orgasm.

This was too much.

It took but a moment.

I silenced her by suffocating her (although detaching that large dyed head from its body would have satisfied me quite a bit more, I must confess). Did I spurt? I would not know.

I do know that during my escape, pursued by her domestics, with their usual stupid (though this time also frightened) air, between the carrying of buckets of water, the smoke, the running, the constant shrieking, and drenched to the skin, I was constrained to jab a letter opener here and there into the abdomens presenting themselves before me; and that the device got stuck in giblets and waistcoats, that I soiled my garments and my hands, that the cries, blood, burning embers, and teetering of bodies and of walls, all necessitated awkward, defensive, rapid changes of course. Enraged, I felt myself going insane.

It was eight o'clock, and I was running late, very (upon disembarking I had sent a note to Sophie with some lilies of the valley: I will arrive this evening at seven). I had to reorganize myself. I had to leave behind that indefinite culmination, that swift destruction. I had to change my clothes. My dependency, my hope were in flames, an ideal concomitant to my purest expectations. I had to reach the back alley, breathe, calculate. I had to, had to . . . Solitude.

I thought back upon the year of separation from Sophie.

Upon my wasted peregrinations.

Upon heartbreak.

It is not true that love is space and time become felt. It is not true that our lives are many, and as many the steps that we take. One possession suffices to complicate us, to scar us.

What an obsession it became when in another I saw her instead. Her, her, Sophie, naked, kneeling between the legs of another, man or woman, at the foot of unmade beds, the snifters of cognac, beautiful fruit, her tousled straw-colored hair with the rude, unknown fingers tangled there, rubbing themselves in it and defiling it with triviality.

Dear Lord, what an obsession those refined lips sculpted by Phidias, crenellated by those teeth of hers and encrusted with the tobacco-stained spittle that gathered around them! Madonna, what an obsession to see her with her mouth open, even splayed wide, crammed with dripping organs while, in a moment of pause, she took a deep breath and then, with impunity, swallowed liters, oceans of horrible gelatin! Misericordia, what an obsession that dazzling cavity, wrinkled, inviting—truly no longer mine—that in the final crisis made her raise her head in vainglory!

One can never forget it.

I had to eliminate her. It was done.

I poisoned her.

Here is the coffee. The story is ended.

I remember—and how could it have escaped my notice?—that in the chamber, as if it were a thing of virtually no importance, there was a breeze streaming through the slightly open windows, which were girdled by fencing made of wrought iron similar to that of this table, and by Canterbury bells that looked as if they'd been frescoed by Tiepolo. Some had a corolla that was deep blue, others one of a rose color exactly like that of the striped skin underneath its winged pedicels. And I, my discontent.

Mermaids, and Other Sea Creatures

Margherita Giacobino

"My love! Finally!" shouted Pina, waving her bare arms as if she wanted to embrace her from up above. Then the window was empty, and the solid sound of clogs rapidly descending the stairs could be heard. Her suitcase at her feet, Anita waited there in the morning sun without moving, slightly dazed, as happened to her every time she arrived. It wasn't easy, and it especially took some time to shake off that other world that stuck to her skin and to her clothes and that was still buzzing, though more and more weakly, in her head. At every new arrival on the island, at least for a few hours, she was still a foreigner. She was here but not completely here, always left feeling somewhat disembodied by the immensity of the journey, stunned by the ocean winds on the ferry. So Pina's embrace caught her a bit by surprise, and she laughed and gasped and was submerged for an instant underneath that wave of warm and cool skin with its smell of bread, of soap, of deodorant, and of sweat.

"Come inside, I'll make you some coffee," said Pina, grabbing the suitcase. Following her in, she felt the need to rest her palm on the stuccoed wall next to the door, as if to reestablish some mute, familiar contact with the house, which was part of the living body of the island.

That evening at dinner, after having placed a bottle of red wine on the table, Pina told her about the latest events of local news: her niece Adele was getting married to the mailman; Caterina the seamstress had gotten into a hair-pulling match in the piazza with Antonietta the prostitute, whom Caterina thought was leading her son astray; the wife of the police chief had fled to the continent with an outsider, but then had returned all contrite, and the chief gave her a good knocking around and then gave her a new necklace with matching earrings; three of Santo's she-goats died, poor fellow, but his wife was pregnant again; and at the end of the island, below Donkey Cliff, a strange woman, half-crazy and savage, had taken up residence, a German.

"You won't believe it, but when I saw her I couldn't even tell if she was a man or a woman. With these amazing muscles in her arms, here," said Pina, swelling her biceps to show her.

"Bigger than yours?" said Anita, inhaling her cigarette smoke with eyes half-closed.

"Mine? What are you talking about?" retorted Pina, who lifted sacks of flour as if they were pillows and who shook the entire house when she kneaded the pizza dough on the table. "This is only flab, feel," she laughed, placing Anita's hand upon her hard, bronzed arms.

"You are gorgeous, Pina," said Anita, laughing. Pina's skin was compact and elastic, and seemed to have the same firm, smooth grain of the handful of eucalyptus trees in the courtyard on the windward side of the house. She would have wanted to say, "I like you, Pina, because I can touch you, and because you laugh loudly; because you don't possess any of that

Margherita Giacobino

guardedness that keeps us at a distance from one another; and because you don't care about keeping your legs together when you're sitting in front of me or about moving your body like some kind of lady." But Pina would not have understood. And furthermore, this was still what Anita the foreigner thought, she who had just arrived and who was still intent upon absorbing, on translating it all, and ultimately on blunting the impact the island had upon her five senses.

The next morning when Anita awoke, she was no longer a foreigner; and over the cup of steaming black coffee, Pina no longer had the effect on her of the previous evening: she was just Pina, in her house, on her island, as she had always been.

It was three days later, while she was coming back from the beach with her wet towel around her neck, that she saw the German woman. She saw her above, standing out against the sky on a black rock ridge, walking alongside a donkey with two swinging canteens slung over its neck. Even though the woman did not appear out of place in that landscape, she knew immediately that it was the German woman, since she bore an air of otherness, of obstinate and wary solitude.

The following day, as she was about to descend to her usual stretch of beach, she offhandedly decided to continue up the path to the grottoes out on the promontory, almost a kilometer further along. It was a place that no one ever went to, hard to reach and solitary, with the naked stone of Donkey Cliff rising above it. And there, as she had expected without admitting it to herself, she found the German woman. It was absurd to have expected it, as absurd as it was to feel a slight heartthrob at the sight of that curved knee raised above that rock leaning toward the sea. She instinctively slowed her pace, as if wanting to come upon her by surprise before she escaped, since Anita thought of her a bit as some kind of wild animal, a dolphin or seal, or maybe a mermaid just emerged from the depths and ready to dive back in.

She spread out her towel in the farthest possible corner of what it would have been an exaggeration to call a beach. It was a hodgepodge of boulders, more or less large and craggy, tumbling into water that was immediately deep, that at barely three meters from the shoreline shaded from deep azure to the blue-green of open sea. After a quick swim, she came back out and sat down on her towel. She realized that the presence of the other, who had apparently not moved, gave time a different consistency: sharp, almost thorny. She also realized that she had nothing to do but shake out her hair like a wet dog and wait until the salt began to tingle on her shoulders as they dried in the sun. Nothing to do but to look over there. From where she was, she could see her whole body, from the head of close-cropped blond hair to the foot dangling in the water, and her entire right side, where the skin, of a pale bronze color, was completely uninterrupted by the cloth or laces of a bathing suit. She was sunbathing naked, the German woman, with her eyes closed, still and stubborn under rays that must have already burned her, since one could see pale colored blotches on her forehead and shoulders. A Saint Joan come to burn in the southern heat, she thought. Masculine, perhaps, compared to the full, dark women of the island—she now appreciated the ambiguity that had played on Pina's imagination—but she saw only the vulnerable and insistent delicacy of her protruding breastbones, of the slender wrists, of the small breasts in that strong, angular body.

"I shouldn't stare, it's rude," Anita wisely said to herself, lowering her eyes and looking at her toes, which restlessly moved on the yellow terrycloth. "She came here to be alone, as I myself did."

A little gray crab skittered quickly past her and disappeared into a crack between two boulders. It was a small, shadowy crevice, rhythmically traversed by the sound of the beating waves, amplified by its rock walls; wedged into a niche inside, a waving ruby-colored creature—mollusk or plant?—was caressed by the water. Anita reached and touched it with her

Margherita Giacobino

finger: it was hard and at the same time soft, like velvet-covered stone.

And she returned to watching the woman on the rock. "Well," she said to herself, "I know that she is there, and she knows that I am here. Might as well stop pretending and introduce ourselves."

The motionlessness of the other was so complete that Anita at first felt vaguely offended, then rejected; then she began to worry. Was she sick? was she alive or dead? No, because in this heat a sunstroke comes quickly, and these hard-headed Nordic types hate to admit any weakness . . . She felt stupid, started to rummage in her canvas bag until she touched the hot metal of her cigarette case. She was about to light one, when the German woman suddenly rolled over onto one elbow and turned directly toward her.

Her eyes were a cold gray color like mountain water, hostile, maybe scared, diffident but at the same time defiant. Anita smiled and struggled to not lower her eyes under such a direct stare, in the face of which a smile of courtesy was so totally inadequate. In an instant, the German woman slid into the sea with the rapidity and grace of a sea creature and disappeared swimming behind the tumbled boulders.

When she returned—how much time had passed? she had left behind her the echo of her presence, like an empty shell still vibrating upon the slanted rock—she climbed back up to stretch herself out under the sun, and Anita read in her gestures, in the calm with which she lay there, a sign of truce, even of acceptance. She felt a light, unmotivated euphoria, which impelled her to dive into the water again herself and to splash about more noisily than was strictly necessary. When she came out again, the German woman had gone. Only her wet imprint on the rock remained.

They met the day after, and the day after that. When it began to seem that the two of them had established a certain routine, which made Anita subtly and unexpectedly happy, one day the woman did not show up, and for two mornings thereafter the rock remained empty. Fortunately, Anita had brought a book, and she lay there on her stomach and read; from time to time, she lifted her head, losing her place, and was distracted listening to the sound of the waves and the shrill humming of the cicadas, and she felt a shiver run through her that might or might not be—she still did not speak to herself of these ever so slight sensations—the distant pleasure of anticipation.

It was at the wedding of Pina's niece that she realized. The awareness did not descend from her head to other, lower organs, but rose from within, from the legs, from the cavities within the belly, from the beating blood, from the part of her more in contact with the hot, rocky earth. In the car carrying them to the church, squeezed between two bridesmaids sweating in flounced cream-colored dresses, she felt herself become infused by an exquisite softness at the contact of those two young bodies, restless and anonymous. Vague grazing touches, two arms encircling her in a dance, a hand that lingered a little in hers while giving her a glass, resounded inside of her like the vibrating tones of a gong. The gaze of Antonio over the accordion, tender and allusive, or perhaps only a little foggy with wine, made the image of that summer—was it eight years ago? ten?—flash intermittently across her mind: when he was a boy with barely a hair on his face, and they met sometimes at night behind the cane-brake, and that adventure, a little bitter and so long ago, sparked now another flame, so similar and yet so different. She had felt it too many times not to know what it was, but acknowledging it always left her breathless, dazed as if by an altogether new moon that had risen in the sky and had plucked the cords of her body's memory, and her mind's, only to better glow in its newness. And the moon was there, in fact, round and bright, when, still at the table, with one of those smiles with which one spoke of sex and childbirth and other merry mysteries, Pina said to her, "You met the German woman." It was not a question, and she replied, "Yes, I met her," and she suddenly felt how insufficient it was to label her "the German woman," and how she wanted to know her name so as to be able to call her by it.

The morning after, she still was not there. Slowly, as if performing an intimate and circumspect gesture, Anita emerged from the water and lay on her rock. The heat of the stone and of the air seemed animate, heat from her body that continued to impregnate that place. She let herself slip into a world of suspended sensations, where absence and presence were almost the same thing, like sky and sea, mixing one into another. And perhaps she became drowsy, dangerously, because she did not notice her arrival until, alerted by a rustle, she jerked her head around and saw two tanned legs covered with fine blond hair standing next to her. The German woman looked down at her with what, from below, seemed like an enigmatic and vaguely ironic air. She quickly sat up. "I'm sorry. I've stolen your spot. I'll move."

"No, no," said a voice that was surprisingly sweet, low and a bit gravelly. She must not have had many opportunities to speak, the German woman. She sat down a little farther off and began to slowly, thoughtfully, slip off her tee shirt.

"So, we've switched roles. Now it's my turn to be here exposed, on view," Anita thought with her eyes closed, and the fact actually hardly bothered her. There is a certain pleasure in being watched, when you want to be, a pleasure that is stronger than shyness and embarrassment and the knowledge that you are no longer twenty years old. And she gave herself over to it, with a certain trepidation, conscious that this also involved a certain testing of her, and she of herself. The sun ignited her closed eyelids with a liquid flame. She thought of the ruby clutching the rock and caressed by the waves, soft and dense like a clot of blood, slightly concave in the center, and she felt a quiver run along her legs.

"And if she is *not* watching me after all?" she then asked, because she was a practical woman, and couldn't prevent herself, even in her moment of abandon, to cast a glance toward reality.

But the woman was looking at her, in fact. The woman blushed, as if she had been caught in the act, and smiled a wrinkled half-smile; it seemed as if it were the first time she had smiled in years and years. Then, having obviously had enough of that, she brusquely stood up and dove in. Anita followed her.

After the swim, while they were coming back to stretch out again on the rocks, she said, "My name is Anita. And yours?"

The German woman seemed to hesitate, as if loathe to reveal a secret, and then, "Ursula," she said, with that voice so low and mellow.

Anita told her that she was lodging with Pina, the bread-baker. That she had come here almost ever year, for a long time now. Ursula revealed slowly, as if overcoming some internal resistance, that she lived in an old house under Donkey Cliff.

"I know," said Anita, inhaling a mouthful of cigarette smoke, "I saw you, you and your donkey, the other day."

They spoke a bit in Italian, a bit through gestures, helping each other with the occasional word of English. Suddenly, Ursula brusquely stopped speaking, as if the effort of communicating had exhausted her, and she looked at Anita almost with hostility. She was not naked this time, but had kept on the bottom part of an old blue bathing suit. Anita felt herself begin to tremble under that gray glare. She would have wanted to say, "Look, it's easy. All you need to do is let yourself go. Don't you see that I like you?" But Ursula would flee headlong. And, of course, one could always be mistaken.

Anita pulled out her sun tan oil and began to rub it onto her arms. "Do you want some? Aren't you afraid of getting burned?" And since she got no response, Anita poured some into her palm and massaged it into the hard, contracted muscles of Ursula's shoulders. How many times in her life had she ever found herself playing mama to someone a little, just a little, because any more than that would have been impossible for her; *she herself* would have fled headlong. And yet she could

Margherita Giacobino

never seem to avoid doing so, perhaps because she always found herself with, or chose, people younger than herself. But people of her age were as if dead and embalmed, mummies— how can mummies inspire desire? she asked herself, as the muscles beneath her hands gradually relaxed, and Ursula's head yielded and dropped forward.

"There we are. Now you can do the rest yourself," she said, tossing the oil into her lap, and tersely breaking the fragile spell. "Now it's your turn," she thought. "I can't do everything."

Ursula came to her senses as if from a dream, then gave the tube back to her. "I don't need this," she said darkly.

"You know that your name fits you," she said to her before leaving, "Ursula, like the bear, a big she-bear, kind of clumsy, with claws and soft hair . . . Ursula," and she affectionately mussed her hair. "You won't take it personally, will you?"

And Anita disappeared before hearing the response. No matter, since she probably didn't even understand. Or maybe she did.

The island, during that period, tormented her. Sweetly, it's true, a torment that it was hard to complain about, but a torment nonetheless. During the day it was the smells, those intense and shameless smells, the unnerving scent of flowers, pungent aromas of herbs, saline odor of cordage, of fish, a sudden reek of rotting flesh, the hot stench of animal skins in the sun, and again flowers, again salt, earth, fish. It drove her crazy. In the evenings, while playing cards, she would suddenly stop while about to lay down a card, overwhelmed by the nocturnal perfumes and by the magnificence of Pina's massive tits; by the vitality of her smile, her black eyes, her full lips with the slight moustache above them; by the aching and banal beauty of the trembling track of moonlight on the sea; by the intensity of a desire that seemed, at any moment, as if it could make a lover's body materialize right before her eyes and beneath her hands. "What are you doing? You have the ace, and you're not playing it?" Pina asked her, with that smile to whose multiple dimensions of meaning Anita had blindly decided to entrust herself without any longer wondering what lay behind it.

Someone was climbing down the mule path. Shading her eyes with her hands, Anita looked up a moment before the two figures, one human and one not, came to a halt. "Anita! Anita!" shouted a hoarse voice, which broke perhaps out of emotion, perhaps because it was not accustomed to shouting. When Ursula reached her, she was smiling. She was as if transfigured, happy, in command of herself up here, on her own territory. Or perhaps the presence of the donkey reassured her.

"How's it going?" said Anita, breathlessly. "Did you find another beach, or don't you feel like swimming these days?" she wanted to add. But that was precisely what she knew she shouldn't say.

"Come see my house," said Ursula, and she took her hand, dragging her bodily up along the path.

"She's slow," Anita thought as she plodded along panting at Ursula's side. "She swims fast and scampers up cliffs like a mountain goat, but she is slow, and that explains everything."

The house, which had lain empty for many years, seemed at first glance to still be so. It would have required a much more careful examination to be able to tell that the ancient heap of stones was now habitable, or at the very least, inhabited. Ursula was as proud of it as if it were a palace, and Anita, when her eyes adjusted to the semidarkness within—it was almost evening, but not yet time to light the kerosene lamp— saw with what care the few pieces of furniture had been arranged on the freshly washed brick floor, and the pencil drawings hung on the walls.

Outside, in the small parterre standing in front of the house, with her bare feet in the loose black earth of the garden, Ursula pointed out her plants one by one, with shy pride. A rustle behind her made her turn. On the only tree that was growing up there, an elongated crack rapidly descended, and then stopped abruptly, anchored to a branch that gently bounced.

Fascinated, Anita stood staring at the snake that swayed ever so slightly as it hung suspended from the branch. Ursula's arm encircled her shoulders with the same lightness. The snake was black against the red, violet, and indigo sky. The heat of Ursula's arm and of her side pressed against Anita's made her legs go lax, and she leaned upon her, without will or thought, seeking the contact. The snake fell to earth like a ripe fruit, slithered and vanished into a mound of stones next to the furrows, leaving behind a long, elegant S in the dust.

And when the echo of this silent movement was also extinguished (Anita could think of nothing at that moment but the beauty of the snake), Ursula put her arms around her. Much larger and taller, she completely wrapped herself around her, in an embrace in which Anita could feel the pent-up energy, and pressed her cracked, impatient lips to hers. Anita understood that she shouldn't do anything—indeed, she couldn't—and she let herself be explored. Ursula seemed to want to nuzzle every part of her. She felt Ursula's hot breath upon her hair, her eyelids, her neck, while a hand cradled her nape, lovingly, inflexibly. What she had then done, afterward, thinking back on it, she had no idea: she seemed to remember having adhered to the body of Ursula with the same docility of a climbing vine that puts out all over itself tiny, airy tendrils, like little fingers, that clasp onto everything around them. And she no longer thought with her head but with her skin, on which big, soft circles of heat and desire expanded, from her damp face offered up to the searching mouth of Ursula, to the small of her arched back, with its deliciously taut muscles, to her toes spread and immersed in the hot earth.

When Ursula released her, she tottered as if she were drunk. She saw her, so near, breathing heavily, with her shirt unbuttoned—it must have been her—her stormy eyes overflowing, like a flooding river after the spring thaw. And a thought flashed across her mind like lightning: "This is too romantic, too beautiful—the sunset, the snake, the horizon opening toward the sea—and the beauty, when one has shed the fatuousness of youth, becomes muddled, causes pain—I am old enough by now to endure it, she no, she isn't yet." And she hoped that something very prosaic would happen, that the donkey would bray, or let fall a steaming pile of dung, so as to break the evil spell of that incorporeal beauty that had distracted her lover from her body. But the donkey stood staring at her meekly, or sarcastically, without moving, and Ursula turned slowly and passed her hands over her face as if to wash away the kisses, emotions, and who knows what memories or fears.

They started walking, without looking at each other, around the garden, which seemed to have shrunk in size, was now too small for the both of them. While she was pulling out by main strength an onion that refused to let itself be uprooted, Ursula, with her head turned away, said: "You stay here, maybe, tonight?"

"An entire night!" Anita thought, conflicted and a little afraid, as if she had said "I love you" to her. And then she thought of Pina, who would surely worry, and would maybe send people out to search for her, and the gossip that would have ricocheted from one end to the other of the island. But what seemed more plain to her than all this was the idea that now was not the moment, that perhaps one night would not be sufficient to mend the threads broken during the sunset. And the idea of mending them herself, patiently, in the darkness, did not appeal to her.

"I can't," she said, "not tonight. Pina is expecting me. Another time, maybe. Who knows." And she smiled her sweetest smile, as if in reparation.

Ursula turned to look out at the distant light of a boat that trembled on the sea.

"But we'll see each other tomorrow, no?" Anita said, as if nothing had happened. She went home slowly, walking along the path, waving several times as she went, while the other, bent forward, furiously hoed the ground massacring onions.

That evening Pina scolded her for not eating. There were

Margherita Giacobino

fresh grilled sardines, and the scent of garlic was intense, like that of lost love. In bed, she tossed and turned for a long time, cursing the family, which reconstituted itself everywhere one went. Why hadn't she gone to stay in a hotel? she asked herself over and over, feeling Ursula's hands again on her back, on her buttocks, on her neck, and knowing that no solitary remedy would be possible in her exhausted state.

The next day she waited patiently. She was also prepared to wait the day after, and the day after that, because by now she had grown stubborn. However, perhaps as a way of punishing herself, she had forgotten her suntan oil, and she was beginning to get burned, when finally, very late, after the sun had already made the circuit of the promontory, she heard the sound of footsteps.

Ursula arrived like a hurricane, pursued by a small avalanche of stones. And without even deigning to glance at her, she removed what little she had on and threw herself into the water. Anita followed her, trying to keep herself from laughing out loud out of happiness. And she continued to follow her until she no longer had the strength to swim, and then stopped, exhausted and out of breath. A blond head in the distance appeared and disappeared in the blinding blue of the sea. The shore seemed very far off. "And if I were to begin to drown, would she come and save me?" she asked herself doubtfully. But she saw her coming back, swimming with long, regular strokes. And she followed her again, staying close to the rocks on the other side of the point; Ursula turned from time to time to make sure that she was there, and Anita, with her heart pumping hard, thought that women are all Turandots, specialists in cruel trials of love.

Finally, Ursula stopped, hanging onto a narrow tongue of rock, and waited for her. She really did look like a she-bear, rippling and running with water, with her wet hair clinging to her head, her small pointed breasts erect, and that other blond hair between her legs waving like seaweed in the current.

Anita then saw where she had led her: they were at the entrance of one of the grottoes that opened out to sea along that stretch of coastline. It was a large mouth, half-closed and toothed; once inside, she found herself in a blue-green penumbra, a chamber of living stone that had as its floor a mirror of immobile water, and on one side, for a couch, a large boulder, smooth and flat. Arabesques of reflected light shimmered on the walls, and the rippling of the water's surface was faint like the far-off tinkling of a silver bell.

"So, this is your grotto," said Anita.

"It is so beautiful," she went on, "it's intimate, it's luxurious, it's . . ." She didn't complete her sentence, but instead slipped out of her bathing suit and hung it on a spur of rock. And she remained like that, naked on the large, warm, emerging mass of stone. There inside, the bathing suit seemed almost like an offense to that place. On her knees, Ursula cast a long glance toward her, then lay face down and buried her head in her arms.

Anita slid slowly to her; inch by inch she drew next to her. She lightly caressed her back, first with the back of her hand, then with the palm. She traced a small scar, ran her finger along the contours of her buttocks, then measured their roundness with her open hand. What did she want, the German woman, engulfed in her muteness, while her skin rippled in long shivers under Anita's fingers? Did she want tenderness, forcefulness, or maybe long, excruciating anticipation? And why in hell did she herself have to wonder and worry so much, when she was about to burst open from desire like a ripe fig?

"How nice it is in here," Anita began to say again, patiently, stroking her back ever so lightly with her hand, "and after having gotten fried in the sun, and swimming until we were bone tired, look, here it's even better. You feel that laziness, that well-being, that feeling also of having escaped, and being ready for new dangers, or new pleasures, which could be almost the same thing . . ."

"She couldn't have fallen asleep?" she wondered, lifting a hand that fell back, inert. She sighed.

"And I could tell you some things about myself," she went on after a pause, "for example that I have a son, grown up, and that I know how to play pinochle, but do you care? And maybe you would tell me that you came here to find yourself, or to forget someone, a love affair, a disillusionment, I don't know, and that you only love your donkey, you're happy just to be with him, or her, I didn't look, I'm sorry, and that the two of you go every morning to get water . . ."

All of a sudden, Ursula turned over upon her, with her mouth clamped tight. But while she gripped her tightly, immobilizing her under her weight, Anita could see that her eyes were laughing between the pale-colored eyelashes encrusted with salt. And so she too laughed, gurgling, half-suffocating under a voracious kiss and by arms that now squeezed her so hard it hurt. It was almost a battle, one body against another, playful and terribly urgent on the stone surface smooth as paper, and this time Anita did not restrict herself to offering herself to the other, and she no longer wondered to herself. And just like the way the snake had fallen off the branch, quickly, furrowing the air of that sunset, Anita suddenly felt a prolonged spasm of pleasure plunge inside of her, while she squeezed Ursula's muscular thighs between hers. And because of that sudden, almost gratuitous explosion, she let out a cry of surprise, just a fraction of an instant before the two of them, entwined, slipped off the rock into the water.

They pulled themselves out sputtering and laughing and shaking their hair, and she asked, "Did you hurt yourself?" because a drop of blood was welling on Ursula's foot.

"Nothing. A sea urchin," she replied, pulling Anita to herself.

But Anita bent down and sucked away the blood on her foot. Then, delicately, she kissed it. Ursula's arms were again around her, and notwithstanding the virtual sunstroke, the swim, and the joyful exhaustion that had struck her a few moments before, Anita felt newly full of energy. And she needed it because, as she told herself, once others forget about your age, they forget about it completely, and ultimately that is how it should be.

THE NIGHT OF
CROSSED DESTINIES

Silvana La Spina

Marco,

this typed letter will never be signed. Therefore, you will futilely search for me. You will futilely imagine that you know who I am, but who I am is unimportant.

It is enough for you to know that I saw you by chance the other day. You passed right in front of me and didn't even look at me, but I . . . I understood everything. You don't know it, but I have known you for some time, yes, before ever meeting you I knew of your existence. There are certainties in life that cannot be erased, however much one wants to. At the very most, one can suffer a lapse of faith—did I really, in fact, meet you? did I ever see you on that day? But then there you were, pushing a supermarket cart and wearing a sea-green pullover. At that moment, I didn't immediately recognize you, but then you turned and I understood.

I can't say exactly how long it is that I have been waiting for you—years, moments, forever really.

You have never seen me, and therefore you don't know that I have been following you. Now I know where you live, what your name is in this life; of the other life, where we were surely passionate lovers, I don't have any memories, but it must have been somewhere, in some corner of the universe that was in that moment sublime. I've always known it, have you?

Marco,

I heard from your doorkeeper that you tried to find out who it is that has been asking about you. Don't do it, it's pointless. I haven't been the one asking questions about you, but another person on my behalf; therefore, you will never in any way be able to find me out. Why have I done this? I have my reasons. And they are reasons such that I will never allow anyone else to discover them.

Yesterday, I saw you at the window. You were laughing and talking to someone else in the room, but for a second you turned as if you knew that I was watching you. Was it perhaps for this reason that you left the window open? There was a woman with you, I know, I understood that, perhaps even a young and beautiful one. I wasn't able to catch a glimpse of her except in profile, and a profile doesn't reveal very much. The two of you went into the other room, and I followed you—there, too, you left the window open.

Then you began to undress. It's strange, I didn't feel any jealousy, even though I knew the two of you would make love almost immediately. What mattered to me was seeing you naked. I saw you, in fact, from behind. I recognize the blond hair on your lower back and that scar on your right buttock and, when you turned sideways, I saw your member erect and throbbing. Yes, I recognized your member by its slight curved form, which facilitates penetration. But you too, you too, must also have felt something—but what? a memory? a gaze from outside following your every movement? But then you shook your head as people do when absurd thoughts enter their minds, and you returned to her, to that woman.

Silvana La Spina

This time I didn't have the courage to continue to watch the two of you, and yet you left the window open again and if I had wanted to I could have heard your moans. Did I moan too in that other life? did I also groan like a wounded beast whom your member sought to satiate?

Marco,

I know that you are distraught. I read it in your eyes the other day, when I saw the doorkeeper give you my last letter— I, too, was there, but as usual you did not notice me. I know that these days you are having difficulty with work. That is why I am putting some money in with this letter. I don't want you to take any from the others; I don't want you to be humiliated by other women, even if they say to you, "It is a loan, dear, I don't think of it in any other way."

Your lover is, as it turns out, a rich woman—I know even this, as you see—and her money comes from her husband, a vulgar man, I found out, as she herself is vulgar, notwithstanding the Fendi furs and the sophisticated lingerie made of Spanish lace. She is a vulgar woman, I tell you, a common woman. She has been the lover of other younger men—I've investigated thoroughly, you will note—only for the thrill of feeling like a free and promiscuous woman.

But that is not even it. She is merely an egotistical woman who uses sex with the same recklessness as a bitch running to find a tree to urinate on.

Soon even you will understand this—I beg you in the meantime not to let yourself be swallowed up in her desires, not to let yourself be humiliated by her bitch's lust.

You are sensitive, and sensitivity is a gift, not a punishment or an affliction. Were you also like that then? in that other life?

Marco,

I saw you yesterday at the window with your absent gaze interrogating the emptiness—or was it me that you were searching for? me only? Now that you know that I can see you at all times this bewilderment comes upon you.

Unless you want only this: for me to see you, for me to follow you throughout the day, because all this excites you now.

Yesterday, for example, after she had left, you sat down on the couch in the corner, the one underneath the Klimt drawing. You put something on the turntable—something vaguely sacred, so it seemed to me, maybe Bach—and you slowly undressed.

So slowly it was to die for. Then, naked, you turned toward the wall, and you wanted your shadow to stand out sharply against the background, and I saw . . . well, you know what. At the end you were heaving as if you were really with me, inside of me. And now I know that you finally desire me, you want me, for yourself. And this having and not having me let the beast slowly come out of you, the one that is in us all. And the beast is not so much sex, but the indulging with another being in the very same beastliness that pursues us all, that waits in that hidden place in the depths, from which we fear our whole lives that it will arise, and yet we want it to so much.

Suddenly, the ring of the telephone interrupted that moment. Or maybe not? You in fact did not even pick up the receiver. Instead, you remained standing in front of the window staring outside, into the darkness, searching for me.

Marco,

I don't know what's happened to you these days. I haven't been home, and I went to a place that I don't intend to reveal to you—a very sad place unquestionably, but one not worth speaking further about.

One night, however, while I was there, I dreamed of you. The evening before, I had read Borges's story about the Minotaur. And in my dream you were the Minotaur. I saw you unhappily lowing at the moon, to whose divinity you appealed,

Silvana La Spina

to the goddess Luna toward whom you raised your big bull's head and bellowed your unhappy man-beast's song.

I was near you, wearing a peplos like an ancient priestess or a virgin consecrated to holy sacrifice. Yes, maybe that is it. Maybe I was one of the virgins to be sacrificed to you, but not so much to you as to the lunar goddess. You wanted me to kneel before her power, but then I realized that I was kneeling before your power.

And your heart, commingled with that of the beast you were, made you different from other men. You were the man-beast that every woman desires to know; perhaps for this reason women cloak themselves to such an extent in their oft-proclaimed modesty, otherwise they might have to reveal their own unfathomable bestialities, those that men generally disavow (are we not more than any other being made of earthy substance? maybe this accounts for why we give birth and have humors and intuitions that strike fear into you men?).

While you, my dear beast, howled at the moon, or asked its blessings, your member rose in the darkness, becoming larger and more incommensurable, until the night itself became entirely made of your bellowings and your immense member. There was nothing else beside that, except for your furious bestial need manifesting its grandiose virility. Singular. Regal.

At that moment, I was prepared to be sacrificed—now I can understand the myth of Pasiphaë. I bowed down like a beast before you, so you could take me and kill me without pity (no, it was not pity that I wanted, as much as your satiating me and my being satiated).

Marco,

a week after my last letter I saw you slowly climbing the stairs, as if you were sleepwalking. You were carrying a package, and for the first time when you came in you went right to the window and, addressing me, you showed me the package. Then you left—you did it on purpose, didn't you?

I waited a long time for you, and you returned very late—from what infamous places, from what unfathomable abysses did you come that night? Don't ever tell me, I don't want to know. Certainly there had to be a reason for your having been away so long. Then, I understood. The package on the table contained some drug. I followed your every preparation, which I could never have imagined to be so complicated. I saw you lie there at length awaiting the effect. Finally you put Bellini's ballad "Casta Diva" on the turntable. It was then I understood what the package contained.

Where you found that mask I do not know, perhaps in some shop in the old quarter of town, with a leering shopkeeper with sweaty hands inside who, watching you, beautiful as an archangel, felt the need for you to like him and smiled at you with the ruined smile of an old pederast. And perhaps he brazenly asked you, "What do you need it for?" And you just looked at him with empty eyes.

But ultimately it doesn't matter. What matters is that you found it, the head of the Minotaur. I felt a shiver of pleasure: all this was for me, for me.

Marco,
    this is the way it should be. Now you finally understand.

Because it is just. I discovered you, I revealed you to yourself. And now you are mine.

Not in vulgar men's sense of possession, but that kind of reciprocal belonging to a world of desires that all of us contain in ourselves and of which we live in virtual horror.

I have to reveal to you that I come from a strange land, where there is something savage in the air, always; even our sun is a blasphemy. That is why the Church, when it finally achieved dominance over us, taught with still greater force little else but sackcloth and prayers. Had the Benedictines and Franciscans not yet seen the stone phalli at the entrances to our farms? had they been present at the dances of the peasants of the Girgenti? or at the magic circles of the sorceresses who live near Pantalica? had they never seen Segesta?

And were our devoutly pious matrons so devout after all? Do not our gorgeous female saints, with their carved breasts or their vacant eyes, arouse one more than others do? And our churches, our palaces of that funereal baroque that smells of death, what abysses of wormlike life do they contain? And our triduums, our novenas, our Good Fridays with a half-naked, beautiful Christ who wanders the streets followed by weeping women, what do they represent?

And now I understand that wherever we go we carry the flavor and the odor of that land upon us. For this we are so . . . so different. Oh, not in the physical sense, this no, but in the soul, we are murky, dissipated, imbued with a desperate, sickly sensuality (but is it not that way, is not the real sensuality always like that?).

Marco,

don't do it again. Trying to rebel is futile. It is futile to refuse the pimping hand of the doorkeeper when she hands you one of my letters. You did finally take it. Finally, after leaving it on the table for three days without opening it, you could no longer resist.

And now you are reading it, and every now and then you lift your astounded gaze to see if I'm watching you. I am watching you, my dear, and I am infuriated with you for not having opened it immediately.

I'm enraged because you are my slave, the slave of my and your desires, and like every slave you gnaw at your chains. But he who is the slave of himself will never be free, and I instead want to free you from the ancient enslavement to the desires.

I know everything about you, don't forget it. I know that you are an orphan and grew up in the care of a devout aunt who wanted to make a priest out of you—even piety has its egotisms. I know that you spent two years in seminary and that you then fled. I also know why: the prefect fell in love with you and tried in every way to entice you. Forgive him, Marco, love is blind, always, even when it destroys.

I know that to master his fevered desire he had the whole fellowship perform miracle plays, and that during one of them he had you dressed as Lucifer, the angel of damnation. And I know that the following evening he called you to his room and, handing you the gleaming vestments, said, "Do it for me, become again Samaele the accursed one." And when he once again beheld your sinister beauty, he broke into tears and fell to his knees at your feet, begging you to love him.

Yes, my beautiful demon. I know that you have kept those articles of clothing—your abyss, Marco, do you not also see what abysses your heart contains? And now I tell you: dress yourself again as you were then, wear again the robes of the angel of temptation and gaze upon me as you then had to gaze upon your ancient prefect: with malice and fear, but also with the sense of power that comes to you most perfect ones when someone loves you with a love resembling adoration.

And then with those gigantic wings of an angelic demon, come to me in the night and burn with me every lustful desire of yours.

Marco,

I don't want it. I don't want you so anxiously to try to spot behind which window, among all of the windows directly opposite yours, I hide myself and watch you. It's fruitless, for us it could even be fatal. And then, those windows correspond to so many apartments that it is almost impossible to orient oneself, as it is also in your apartment block.

But you just the same wanted to violate the rules of our game—they were my rules, actually, but you were constrained to accept them. So yesterday I even heard your voice in my hallway.

You probably saw Silvia, the prostitute who in her heart still nurtures the dream of love; you probably saw Colonel Arriva, who was with Rommel in the African campaign, but you probably did not grant him time enough to tell you his story. You were searching for me, me alone. You probably saw Signora Rossi Durante, who was in her day a great opera singer, and even now at times I can hear the muted sound of her records playing—old artists are such pathetic creatures.

And you might even have seen me, but this you will never know for certain.

I could be the divorced blonde on the third floor with the cigarette hanging from her lip and the decadent face—that's how you imagine me, isn't it? Or Marika, the daughter of Lula the masseuse. Despite her mother, Marika is an extremely good girl, too bad she was born blind.

Therefore, my dear, don't come looking for me. Instead, dress yourself this evening once again in your betraying angel's robes, or maybe only the wings, my luminous butterfly. Make your body shine in the light of the moon, tonight there is a full moon. Raise your member as straight and high as the sword of he who led the celestial armies.

Marco,

is it true? Are you wondering how a creature like myself can content herself with living a dream (or a delirium)?

And yet you must admit that you have never, never, lived an experience so exciting, and don't you believe that the same is true for me?

In any case, it is not enough for you, I know. Dreaming is never enough for men.

I understood this yesterday evening when the young girl knocked at your door. Is this your new lover, a girl? She was the daughter of the doorkeeper, and she came to do lessons with you in what, English? German? Lust?

She was so pathetic, little Matilde, with her books and notebooks, and you . . . you pretended to be so accomplished.

So that little girl is the new moth, my monstrous spider, our moth, I should say. Since it is for me that you had all that patience, for me that your hand caressed her back at such length. When will you take her? today? tomorrow? next week?

When will you place her hand on your groin so she can know its consistency? And she, the child, what will she say? She is thirteen years old, don't forget.

Marco,
it went as I had predicted. The flesh has its own laws; lust makes its inviolable demands.

The child at first sobbed, but you, my patient spider, you finally won.

I hate you for this, Marco, or perhaps I love you. Did I not lead you on to it, did I not teach you to satisfy the beast?

Marco,
that is it. You've won.

Now, listen. This night, which for the Orientals is a sacred night, the night of crossed destinies, I will knock on your door. I will enter your room and kneel at your feet.

You will have to remain with eyes closed. With eyes closed you will touch my body, which might be young or very ancient. But just the same you will feel a skin that you have never before felt. My hands will then caress you, my long serpent's hair will run over your body. Your nipples will tremble, your member will rise as potent as the Tower of Babel. At that moment, you will think of only one thing: of the profound inner chamber of my being. And when you reach it, something in you that you have never before known will explode. But until then wait, my dear, wait . . .

Marco Vigneri waited all night for the fulfillment of the promise. He put a Bach sonata on the turntable, then a string quintet, then an ancient chant of accompaniment to dervish dances. He was naked, and toward dawn he felt a dark shiver penetrate him. He rose, dressed himself, and went down to the café to get coffee.

The day was gray, but there was a strangely clear sky in the distance. A woman next to him was speaking to the barista about a neighbor of hers who had died that same night, around dawn. And yet, until a day or two ago, she came and went often, and at times could be heard typing.

To whom, one couldn't help but wonder, since she was almost ninety years old. Old people are so strange, she added.

THE ZIPPER

Dacia Maraini

I am trying to remember some emotions from the literature of eroticism. An intense piece from *Little Fadette* by George Sand comes to mind, something I read when I was less than ten years old; I think of Odette's dressing gowns of "crêpe de Chine" that Swann catches a glimpse of; the Song of Songs comes to mind, with its sensual fields of wheat, its grapes and golden lions; I also think of the little purple foot that Tanizaki dreams of carrying with her to her grave. And another foot comes to mind: that of the dead Nastasia Filippovna, tenderly sticking out from under the winding sheet while the charming Prince Myshkin and the insane Rogozhin, both drunk with love, debate.

Eroticism, it seems to me, is something hidden, something that doesn't come out, doesn't let itself be discovered. In those places where it announces itself, where it is put on view and put on sale, it is not to be found . . . So as to appear later, even slyly, in a place where no one expected to seek it, ambiguous and crafty, furtive and fitting.

Eroticism certainly does not consist in the redundantly displayed coitus that one finds in pornographic magazines. There it elicits only yawns and mechanical acts of masturbation.

Eroticism is elsewhere. But where? I think of the unforeseeable, the unexpected, of those moments in which the imagination lets itself go, as if out into warm water, and turns and sees the lights of the shoreline sparkling before it and feels a sense of uneasiness and glorious euphoria.

I am unable to think of anything less erotic than prefabricated eroticism. The sites of eros fly a white flag. Precisely because sensuality is not programmable. It has a cat's temper, and decides in its own good time when and how to make its next appearance.

I remember a time that I attended a costume rehearsal at the theater. And the actors, vexed and vain, passed continually this way and that before the mirror followed by the seamstress with pins in her mouth.

An actor whom I had known for years and with whom I had never exchanged a look that was anything less than professional, asked me to help him zip up his costume in the back.

While I did it, lovingly, as I would have done with any other actor, I felt my fingers burn. My maternal act was transforming itself into something unexpectedly sweet. My cheeks grew hot and my ears icy cold.

So it is that Eros—that strange chubby child born some say of Aphrodite and Ares, while others maintain him to be the progeny of Iris and the angry West Wind—lets fly his arrow in the midst of an ordinary and innocent gesture. The pale flesh under the heavy brocade was beginning to leaven. Intuition told me that he too was feeling the very same unexpected and surprising emotion.

We did not look at each other. My hands only tarried a second or so longer than was necessary on that dry, taut back.

Furthermore, the man that I loved was there, seated next to me. He, too, was an actor. He was trying on his tights for the part of the prince that he was playing.

I had never betrayed him. We were so happy together. And yet the serpent of temptation had ignited my hands, and I felt them begin to caress that half-naked back that offered itself so tentatively to my touch. He would have wanted me to linger as I pulled up that zipper, slowly and more slowly. He would have wanted me to stumble, to breathlessly hang on his neck in that mute and miraculous desire. I would have wanted it, too.

But Iris is a stern mother and requires order in the sentiments. Therefore, with my ears still cold and my cheeks still burning, I put my hands back in my pockets, and I returned to my playwright's chair. From my mouth came only a small inaudible sigh of resignation. Wisdom appeared before my eyes with their dry eyelashes, and my hands remained idle.

I swear I have not written these lines in order to encourage self-denial. I have not renounced other occasions. I wanted only to show how eroticism is timid and insolent and how it can appear when one least expects it to lay upon one its "natural" claims. It is not always wise to renounce. When one is in love, one must at least try.

B o d y

Sandra Petrignani

She is she, a woman. He, an old friend. Many years previously they shared a long love affair.

He—Why do you want to leave him?

She—To give a sense of heroism to my life.

He—I don't understand. Don't you love him anymore?

She—I'm incapable of separating desire and love. For me they are the same thing.

He—You no longer desire him?

She—I still desire him.

He—And so?

She—But I told you: I want to give a sense of heroism to my life. To suffer by imposing suffering upon myself.

He—You say that you desire him. You say that you want to leave him. You say that you want to suffer. But why?

She—Because it's not enough. The body. His body gives me sensations of regressing that frighten me. Last night we slept together. He falls asleep with his arms around me; he squeezes me in a vise. His breathing so close to me prevents me from sleeping. I lie awake. Last night our embrace was even tighter. He fell asleep kissing me, and our lips remained touching. I held his upper lip and he, my lower lip. He seemed like a baby who'd drifted off to sleep while sucking his mother's nipple. I, too, felt small; I was a newborn, too, protected by the maternal body.

He—It must have been lovely.

She—Then his sleep grew deeper. Little by little he detached himself from me. I lost his lips. His body drifted away. Our arms unclasped. I understood the anguish of infants when adults cease to hold them tight and lay them alone in their cribs.

He—But you fell asleep too at a certain point.

She—Yes.

He—His body was there in any case, next to you. Wasn't this reassuring?

She—Yes.

He—When you awoke he was still sleeping?

She—Yes. I woke up very early. His body was there, asleep. Naked. I took his sex in my hand. It was hard.

He—He was dreaming of you.

She—I touched it lightly, so as not to wake him, but he was awake. He was only pretending to be asleep.

He—He wanted to prolong your caresses.

She—But then he couldn't pretend any longer. He began to move. He came inside of me.

He—Do you like to do it upon first awakening?

She—Yes.

He—With me you never wanted to do it upon waking up. You were always in a hurry.

She—You are talking about in the last years.

He—Maybe.

She—Definitely.

He—Definitely.

So: you want to leave him because you are happy with him?

SHE—I am not happy with him. When one is in love one is never happy. The body always slips away. It is a continual experience of abandonment. Possession is momentary, the rest is only loss and memory.

HE—But if you leave him you will have only loss and memory, no possession.

SHE—Once and for all. Don't you understand that I can't bear having him and immediately after not having him, desiring him, possessing him, and knowing while I possess him that immediately thereafter I will already no longer have him, that I will no longer know anything about him, that he will become totally alien?

HE—But it's not true, it's not like that.

SHE—It is. It is absolutely true. A lover is like a baby; it is the smallest, most needy baby in the world, debased by its body, which can only desire and take pleasure and then immediately mourns the end of pleasure and desires again and pleads, pleads, and feels rejected, because the other possesses a human limit, the limit of the body.

HE—Fine, I agree. It is undeniably so. However, we desire each other, we touch each other, penetrate one inside the other, we exchange fluids. Is this the limit of the body?

SHE—No, the limit of the body is distance, the end of pleasure. And pleasure is always all too brief.

HE—Well then, if you leave this man you must never have another, because any other one will be limited by the body and will only give you pleasure and disappoint you and make you desire him again and cause you pain. You are insatiable.

SHE—That is it. As I told you: I want to give a sense of heroism to my life.

HE—By transcending the limits of the body.

SHE—No, of course. I know that is not possible. If anything, by refusing to force those limits.

HE—I don't believe you. You won't be able to do it. You will never be able to suffocate desire, to do without those nocturnal embraces of his, to not watch over his sleep. You are lost in him, I could hear it in your voice.

SHE—Yes, it is so. I miss him terribly. I am at peace only when in contact with his skin. I need little, you know. To be able to caress his belly with my cheek, to intertwine my fingers with his, gently touch the soft hairs on his arm. In the darkness of the movie theater he always takes my hand and caresses it the whole time, and I get excited thinking about all the other caresses that we will give each other later at home. He carries my hand to his mouth and slides his tongue between each of my fingers all the way down to the cleft. Then he places my fingers one by one into the hot interior of his mouth, gently drawing them out again, and I think about when I will do the same to him, to his sex, when we are alone.

HE—But this is not enough for you.

SHE—While there is this anticipation, yes, it is enough for me. In the darkness of the theater, with my hand buried in his groin, feeling his sex hardening under my touch, and mine beneath me, within, growing damper, sweeter, blossoming, waiting for him, my breast swelling in anticipation of his mouth. Yes, it suffices. Perhaps we won't even make it home. He'll stop the car somewhere in the darkness, and I will open his pants and I will suck him until I drink him in, and I will hold his flavor inside of me, as sweet as the Host, for hours and hours. Is this love? Would you call this love?

HE—I would call it desire. But you yourself said that you make no distinction between desire and love. In order to love, it is enough for you to desire. You have always been this way.

SHE—Yes, I desire him, and there is no pleasure that suffices my desire. This is the way that children love. In the anticipation of having him, I am a child that would never detach her mouth from his, that would be caressed eternally,

Sandra Petrignani

without sleep, without food, without even a moment's separation. An infinite comfort, a motionless suspension of time.

HE—I remember those first months, you never let me sleep. At night, suddenly, you'd awaken me, distraught. You would have bad dreams, you would say that in the morning I would no longer love you. You would want to be comforted immediately, you would want to make love.

SHE—Yes, I remember.

HE—And afterward, you would want me to rock you in my arms until morning, but I would be sleepy and would fall back to sleep without cradling you. And in the morning you would be like a frightened cat who'd gotten caught in the rain.

SHE—You have no idea how much I suffered.

HE—But I couldn't give you any more than that. I loved you, I repeated it constantly. It was never enough for you.

SHE—Men never love enough.

HE—I always thought that once you began to behave more normally, once you began, for example, to sleep soundly through the night without needing me to hold you, you would actually have already stopped loving me. I, however, could not be without you.

SHE—I don't know. I don't know what is normal and abnormal in me. I know that my body is a kind of obstacle, and when I fall in love I wish I could close my eyes and plunge into the empty abyss within me, dragging the other down too. But no one is willing to do it.

HE—But yes. When one makes love that is exactly what one does.

SHE—No.

HE—Yes. Why do you never trust what another person tells you of himself?

SHE—Because words are like the body, like a part of it. They are falsehood.

HE—It's not true. There is a truth of the body. It is the only one that can be verified. The body is there. You touch it, and it reacts. It responds to a caress, or it doesn't respond. The body is truthful. And emotions come from the body. The body is a plenitude, not a vacuum. When you took his sex in your hand as he slept and you felt it hard, you did not just touch a muscle, you touched one of his emotions.

SHE—Do you remember the first time we made love?

HE—Yes.

SHE—We were in that restaurant in the country. We were the only young couple there in the midst of an entire roomful of old people. They had arrived by tour bus, you remember, all those old people. And after lunch the music began. An accordion was playing, like in a French film. They broke into couples and danced. They were so happy. I have never been so happy in my whole life. You asked me to dance and we were the odd ones, we so young among all those old people who didn't pay even the slightest attention to us. While in your arms, I was wanting you and thinking that soon, maybe that same day, when we got back, we would make love, and I was terribly unhappy and envious of those old people. Lucky them, I thought, they are at the end, they no longer anticipate anything and can live only in the present.

HE—Unhappy! What are you talking about? You were as taut as a piano wire. You couldn't wait for me to touch you. You pressed your entire body to mine as we danced. I couldn't stand it any longer. I wanted to throw you to the ground, against a wall, kiss you, come inside you, and I had to keep dancing in the middle of all those people . . .

SHE—Don't you understand? I was afraid of the future. I've always been afraid of the future, of losing the intensity of the moment. You brought me into a field. You didn't even give me time to say yes; I came in your hand even before you finished undressing me. I was completely at your mercy, with no will of my own; you did everything. You have always done everything between us. I always liked this, but it also frightened me. You decided when, how . . . and that day, the first, I needed more tenderness, for you to say you loved me. But I was reeling from that first orgasm with your fingers inside me and I was out of breath and you unbelted your pants, you took your sex in your hands, you thrust it into my mouth, pushing it deep into my throat; I couldn't breathe, you pushed harder, I was suffocating and my stomach was turning. Then you opened my legs and came inside me. What was the need for all that violence? But perhaps it was that violence that persuaded me. I thought then that I would never offer any resistance, that you could do with me what you liked, that I would die if you abandoned me.

He—You always said that the violence of my desire reassured you, that timid guys make you inhibited . . .

She—Yes, it's true. In the face of sex, I like to feel unarmed, lost. It is necessary for all the power to be in the hands of the other. Even the power to toss me aside immediately after.

He—But that is what you can't bear, what makes you go insane with sorrow.

She—Yes, it is so. But that is in the order of things. It is for this reason that I would like to withdraw and to give a heroic sense to my life, to leave my beloved, to love him no longer, to no longer caress him, nor draw near enough to breathe his fragrance. The smell of him . . . just thinking about it is enough to bathe me in vaginal fluids, to produce tiny tremors in me.

He—Stop, you are making me jealous! No, go on, tell me about him. This, too, is a way of possessing you.

She—I want him as one wants food, out of need. It is as if I were so defenseless as to be unable to procure it by myself; only he decides whether to assuage my hunger or to let me die of it. When he is gone, I starve, I am a beggar. No, not really. A beggar has certain resources. I am an infant, totally dependent on the attentions of its mother, on her memory. If she forgets me, my existence, I am lost, I die.

He—How then do you think you can withdraw yourself? An infant does not in any way get to determine its fate. It can only hope that someone else takes it in.

She—Yes, you are right. It is so. I delude myself in thinking that I am not finally so weak as that. But the shape of his mouth is enough to hold me entirely in his thrall.

He—How is his mouth?

She—Eager.

He—He, too, must be weak where you are concerned. He, too, must be in your thrall and afraid of being so.

She—Perhaps.

He—Tell me about his mouth. How does he kiss you?

She—For a long time. He never hurries.

He—Then his is a calm eagerness.

She—Yes, he makes love for pure pleasure, not out of need. He does not need me as I do him.

He—That is your opinion. You always underestimate the strength of feeling of the other.

She—Feeling? Who was talking about feeling? We were speaking only about the body. We adhere only to the evidence, or don't we?

He—Then you admit it. The body is evidence, and a body that desires is a body that loves.

She—For me it is so. But I don't have many desires. I concentrate, usually, on a sole desire. Because, as I've said, it is a question of life and death.

He—Ah, wonderful, wonderful. I long again to be loved like that. What a shame, though, that ultimately you are the one who is saved and you let the other die.

She—What are you saying? Why? It is not true.

He—I don't understand how it happens, but at a certain point you become satiated. You escape from your fantasy of starvation, and you become the one who lets the other starve.

Sandra Petrignani

Without realizing it, because you are unable to imagine that others are hungry for you, too, for your body. You leave it there, like an empty wrapper, the body, and think that the other is satiated. But you have already carried it all away; there is no nourishment left in that simulacrum of yours. I remember quite well the anguish of those days, when I threw myself upon you and you were always somewhere else. What did I have in my hands, in my mouth? An object that didn't love me. I penetrated a mechanical doll that responded to stimuli but blocked the way of emotions, life, everything. Was this "the moment," "intensity"? You don't know what you're speaking of when you speak of the body. When you denigrate it. The body is the person, completely. It is the only medium we have through which we can enter into deep contact with another human being. The word is not the medium. It is the body, the emotion of the body, its intensity. If you take away from the body the intensity of its responses, you offend it and offend other bodies that enter into contact with yours.

SHE—Oh, don't do that, don't say that.

HE—Yes, I do say it. You know only how to be the baby, and the baby grows and separates itself. You don't know how to be the mother, who remains and protects. Who loves.

SHE—But I am the one, I, who needs that mother.

HE—Many years have passed, and nothing has changed. You always want to have it all, too much. But I would still like to be that body that you love now. I would still like to take upon myself the full complement of your absurd desires, to say yes to every request of yours just to see where you would end, if you would end. I would no longer be afraid.

SHE—But I ask nothing. I curl up in the warmth and wait for the caresses. And I never know whether they will come. He ignites easily; he is like a fountain to which all may come to drink. He gets distracted, risks losing me at every turn, and does not even realize it. He will make me die of hunger.

He—He is not a good mother, either.

She—No, he isn't.

He—Is he a seducer?

She—I believe so, if seducers are those who let themselves be easily seduced.

He—It is true, seducers cannot resist enticements. They follow all pathways, they are not able to choose. They are like gamblers: they must bet and bet until they lose everything that they have won.

She—Then he will finally lose me.

He—That is certain. You will be lost, and he will have lost you. It will be dramatic.

She—Oh no. It is not possible. I need his body. When he is near me and not aware of me, I vanish. I come to life if he looks upon me. I can caress him for hours, I can do without orgasm, one touch is enough for me. It is enough just to be there and for him to be there, next to me, aware of me. I feel his body even at a distance; I feel his heat within mine constantly. This is not always the case with me. I have been in love with men that have not made me this giddy. I have not always felt this crumbling, as if my body were dissolving. As if a caress belonged to the air and not to earth and to the concreteness of skin. Sometimes I make love with him without needing to even touch him.

He—You contradict yourself. You said that you need his body and then you said that you can do without touching it.

She—Yes, it is so. We feel together at times, from far away.

He—But how do you know?

She—I know.

He—An umbilical cord?

She—Yes.

He—Communion?

She—Yes, I dreamed that we were taking communion to-gether in a big church. We were of mystical bodiliness. And when I make love with him I cannot free myself of this fantasy: I eat his body, and I offer him mine. It is not exactly a fantasy. We truly do eat each other, and this has no element of cannibalism in it; it is rather a sucking of milk, a primordial feeding. One drinks saliva, blood, se-men. It is no small thing feeding oneself this way upon another, upon his emotions, his thoughts. I try in this way to conquer the limits of the body, to go out of myself for a moment a bit longer than that of the orgasm. We are aggregates of particles; we need to disorder them, stir them up, from time to time. It is true what you were saying: there are sexual encounters with no resonance, there are cold caresses, a pure mechanical pleasure of the body. And then there is the possibility that there is something more, precisely because one can dissolve.

HE—Enough, stop, I don't follow you. Let's go back to the beginning. You told me that last night you slept together and that he fell asleep with your lips between his. And that you then made love as soon as you woke up.

SHE—Yes, it is so.

HE—And how was it? Tell me. Because it was after this that you decided to leave him.

SHE—Yes.

HE—You held his sex in your hand, and he woke up.

SHE—Yes.

HE—And he began to caress you?

SHE—Yes. He forced one of his legs between mine, and he pushed them apart. He licked his fingers and stroked me between my thighs. He slipped two fingers into my vagina, and he thrust them inside of me. Meanwhile, he was lick-ing my breast, kissing my eyes, plunging his tongue into my ears, my mouth. Should I keep going?

HE—He came inside you?

SHE—Yes. He grasped my wrists and he came inside me.

HE—And was he tender?

SHE—Yes, very tender.

HE—He moved gently, or hard?

SHE—First gently, then hard. Then gently, then hard, harder, then very hard. I came at the same time that he did. He waited for me.

HE—It felt good?

SHE—Yes, very good.

HE—Perfect?

SHE—Yes, perfect.

HE—And then?

SHE—Then it was morning. He washed, he dressed, he left. He kissed me before leaving; he held my arms tightly.

HE—And you?

SHE—I stayed in bed a little while longer, trying to conserve his heat.

HE—But he had left.

SHE—Yes, he had left. And for me when he goes, it is forever, forever.

HE—It is because of this that you decided to leave him.

SHE—Yes.

HE—I understand.

SHE—What?

HE—Everything. I understand why you stopped loving me so many years ago.

SHE—Really?

HE—Do you remember *Romeo and Juliet*?

SHE—What should I remember about it?

HE—The scene in which they had spent the night together, and we find out that he must depart at dawn, otherwise they will kill him.

SHE—Ah, yes. And they hear the nightingale sing.

HE—No, they hear the lark, whose song signals the break of day. But Juliet says: no, it was not the lark, it was the nightingale. Because she doesn't want Romeo to leave. "I must be gone and live," he says, "or stay and die."

SHE—And so? What do you understand by this? Tell me.

HE—You too were saying that it was the nightingale, and I was insisting it was the lark. Romeo says to Juliet, Yes, my love, let's talk still, it is not yet day. I, however, went to the window. I opened it, and I destroyed your dream. I let the daylight in.

SHE—Yes, you let the daylight in.

HE—Reality, time.

SHE—"To be gone and live." To save oneself, one must surrender love, sacrifice it.

HE—Today, however, I would stay. "Come, death, you are welcome. Juliet so wishes it."

Y o u   D r i v e

Lidia Ravera

"Do you feel violated?" he asked her, removing his lips from hers. She drew the pads of her fingers lightly along the corner of her mouth: chin, lower cheek. The skin burned; he had not shaved for three days. Did she feel violated?

"Excuse me?"

He was smiling. She smiled. He progressive, she past perfect. She extinguished her smile, his continued.

"It's just that I wouldn't want to undertake anything that you might find, I don't know, invasive, unwelcome . . ."

They were seated on the couch in her law office.

She got up, smoothing her skirt from the waistline down to remove any wrinkles she was imagining, any flattened nap in the velvet.

"Don't go, wait," he said. He grabbed her wrist and was pulling her back down, toward the pillows on the couch.

She sat down, her heart a little heavy, her skin a bit hot,

her mouth a little tired. Not so terrible, if not great; no singing in the blood, no thawing out.

Deliberating, she let herself be kissed again.

This time he was more accurate, less pressure, better aim. She tried to grasp his chest, neither a sporting grip nor a placation, just two hands, one on the right, one on the left of the rib cage. The individual ribs could just barely be made out. His clothes, certainly, the jacket, vest, shirt; but also a firm layer of adipose tissue. Thus it is that the years protect the skeleton. It is a serviceable coating, the direct secretion of time: so that you can never actually be touched. Birds are skinny, bipeds substantial.

He hugged her very hard. She was thin, she knew. It's important that I be the thin one, a fish bone in a Moulinex. Squeeze, squeeze out the juice.

Their noses grazed, risking the comic (the nose is not a serious part of the face; nice to look at if it's beautiful, but you don't touch it, it's not romantic), then settled into position one next to the other, leaving the mouths room to work.

The kiss lasted for minutes and minutes. Minutes are the unit of measure for extemporaneous love.

The secretary could have entered, a tiresome girl, always well-dressed, well-coifed, well-mannered.

Perhaps a variation? She knowingly brushed his ears with her lips, which she detached with difficulty from his cupping-glass kiss.

He registered this progress by tentatively slipping his hand under her sweater. A bold maneuver. She wore no apparatus for containing the breasts. This fact impressed him as a political statement. She liked that about herself, that she was a little untamed, that her head was full of quotations, that she never tired of contriving artificial protractions, of remembering battles, without sense, without by-nows, without warrant.

He considered venturing a favorable comment on the positive consistency of that anatomical part, perhaps relative to age.

Would she be charmed or offended by it?

He discreetly kissed her nipple. He hazarded, "You have great breasts." "Thanks," she said, in a shrill voice.

She pulled away from him and looked at him with a gaze that would not relent. Her eyes, of oriental cut, had been beautiful. Now, folds of skin from her upper eyelids partially covered them, like a censure upon their vitality, and underneath the shadow of a difficult night's sleep ruined their shape. Her eyelashes were long, and if she remembered to put on her mascara one could not help but notice them. But certainly the amatory scuffle had disarranged the makeup. Other than the swollen shadows of her sunken sockets, there was probably also a smudge of black right underneath, like the residue of an erasure.

He held her gaze, but suffered.

He had made a mistake, continued to make mistakes. Behaving well with a woman like Nina, behaving well, courteously, with respect, and above all with love, was a cross for him.

An intelligent woman. But why had he put himself in that situation? The world is full of girls, swarms of young saleswomen with little dreams; there are single women, timid women, warmhearted women.

"Excuse me," he said, and got up, hoping that his roomy pants of heavy fustian hid his lewd erection, that mute and solid request that excites women, but not her, not Nina, or at least Nina, who knows . . .

She had remained seated and was stretching, a merry look in her eyes, which were half-closed upon that light of meek arrogance.

If she would only say something, he would feel better. He lit a cigarette, to give some excuse for his standing there, large, sweaty, uncertain.

"What is it that I have to excuse you for, exactly?"

Nina knew perfectly well that that superior, formal, fuck-off tone of hers would carry her back to a place to which she did not want to return. She felt the key turn in the lock upon the castle secrets—prisoner again, prisoner. She didn't dare raise her gaze and look upon him, and yet she was certain that, under those hateful folds of skin, her defiant eyes gleamed maliciously.

He tried to tune himself back in, with the courage of one who knows he has lost so has no reason not to try.

"Sexual harassment?" he said. His tone was perfect modern comedy.

"Not of any kind I didn't want," said Nina.

She stood up: she barely came up to his shoulders. She passed a hand through her hair. It was so thin, it got dirty so easily and fell into a part on her forehead. She never felt neat, never light and airy.

And now he was on the verge of leaving. She wanted to reassure him, but continued to play the queen.

"I'm horrendous-looking," she said in a low voice. Perhaps show a weakness, the only one she actually possessed. That of not being beautiful. The years, the eyes being gradually eclipsed. "Don't look at me, please, I'm a monster."

He considered the option of embracing her. Standing, he felt stronger. There was a frailness about Nina's body: her shoulders tended to hunch, her small head stuck slightly forward on her neck, a little bird.

He brushed her cheek caressingly. He was afraid the gesture was paternalistic. He wanted to be poetic: "A sad little mussy bird."

Nina touched her hair again.

"It would be better for you to put two ideas out of your mind," she said, "the hearing is tomorrow."

"Do you still need me?" he said.

She opened her eyes exaggeratedly wide. Only then was she sure they were visible.

"In what sense?"

Controlling his desire, clearly inconvenient, to smack that small pale face, blotched here and there with face powder, he replied: "In the sense of our official roles: do you need more information, statements, evidence . . . I've still got a half hour."

Nina moved toward her desk, walking slowly, leading with her pelvis, thrusting her shoulders back. Control. After thirty, spontaneity is risky. Her skirt tightly held her hips; she knew she could still count on her butt.

"Calm down, I'm not going to let them give you life."

Legal protocols, documents: merely touching them gave her a sense of peace, safety.

"I'm the only man getting divorced who is being represented by a woman."

"That's because you're shrewd."

"Shrewd?"

"Hate, competitiveness, knowledge of the species: only a woman can destroy a woman."

She turned with a sheet in her hand. He was very near. His dog's eyes were a little puffy, a little dejected, resigned and needy. The pores on his nose were slightly dilated.

"You have to sign a few papers."

He impetuously grabbed her by the neck and pressed a hard, painful kiss on her mouth, tasting her blood. The papers fell to the floor. Nina moaned, opening her eyes, then closing them, a fish pulled up on dry land gasping for oxygen. He had no idea by what progression of maneuvers he had managed to lay her on the floor.

High and dry. He debated with himself. He felt her move. Under, under.

Her sharp shoulderblades flat on the marble. I'm lying on her, he thought, I'm hurting her, I'm squashing her. He had no intention of stopping. Hands, buttons, he grabbed the belt from her skirt in his fist, actions, actions, hands quicker than thought, feeling her move, something a little brutish, grab the neckline of her sweater, actions, knuckles scraping against her belly, she's moving less now, she's closed her eyes, her butt, slip the hand flat, under, under, the hand becomes pliable, the butt, don't think, panties, he feels the fabric give way, the tearing of nylon, nothing too urgent, she's not moving now, oh Nina, Nina, why is this so difficult, grabbing my thing like a little boy, squeezing it, I'm afraid, lose the possibility of impaling you, pinning you, nude to the waist, in my calendar, in my date book, because the days the days the days, they all border on the end, because they are all contained one within another and there are no doors, nothing opens and nothing closes, nothing assumes order.

He entered her body overwhelmed by a banal anxiety.

To do it quickly, to do it well, to find something to say afterward. He was excited, and in this there was an animal truth somewhat reassuring. He felt her teeth under his lips, the teeth of his lawyer.

"Oh Nina, Nina," he murmured.

"Paolo," she said. It wasn't an invocation.

"A million lire a month in child support is excellent, if you consider your income."

"And plus the fact that I can see the children when I want, that there's a minimum limit but not a maximum, that was truly a master stroke."

Paolo raised the glass of prosecco, his hand poised in mid-air above the little table's round surface of gray marble, and waited for Nina to toast with him.

"I don't like the look with which your wife greeted me. She refused to shake my hand."

"And so why do you refuse to toast with *me?*"

"I'm sorry. I was preoccupied."

The two glasses touch, we don't. The party is already over, Nina thought.

"You're beautiful, Nina, when you are preoccupied."

"You're handsome when you bullshit."

This time they toasted better; a couple of people turned at the noise coming from the adjacent table. They laughed. They drank the glasses down in one gulp. The attention of others is a potent aphrodisiac, the dream of still being able to be envied.

"Waiter," said Paolo, twisting in his chair towards the bar. "Two more."

"Are you crazy? You know I'm getting drunk."

"Good. I'll take advantage of the fact."

"You did that yesterday as well."

"You get into my blood, I can't help it."

The waiter took the empty glasses and placed full ones on the table. The wine was clear, effervescent. In a small glass bowl the olives, in another cubes of cheese, raw carrots all sliced in the same shape.

"This is the one thing I truly miss about Milan," said Paolo, fishing out an olive. "The ritual of the aperitif—the inviting bar, the little indulgence, the nibbling. In Rome there are no nice rooms in the bars; either the sun is out and it's nice weather for it, or it doesn't work. You have to stand, the doors are always open; you're held hostage by grimy young guys who grab the wrong glass. They only drink hard liquor in Rome."

Nina smiled blankly. She's not listening, thought Paolo.

The revelation offended him more than was logical. All of her there was could be found in that faraway gaze, set in a polite attitude of cold, indifferent benevolence.

"You're not listening to me," he said, mastering his annoyance, but feeling the effects of an involuntary self-estrangement. It seems like I'm dubbing myself. Nina shook herself out of it, provocatively, almost as if to give proof of the truth of his accusation. She fixed him with a frank scowl (a woman who never lies, hence a non-woman).

"Do you think it's possible that your wife knows somehow that we had sex, you and I?"

"Do you care?"

"Don't you?"

"No."

Nina shifted her gaze to the world outside the bar's front

window. An entire humanity was there battling against the midday, on a normal Tuesday like any other.

"I care about you," Paolo said.

Nina drew her gaze slowly back to him: a kind thing to say, a phrase that carried within itself a sense of unexpected peace. She felt in debt—it was not a helpful sentiment—to him for this love, and yet it had always made her suffer: brief pangs, cold slaps of recognition, they bowed her down like strong gusts of wind.

"Shall we drink another?" she mischievously raised her glass. Instead, she would have liked to embrace him.

After a long string of passing clouds, the sky grew quite dark, as if night had been grafted into day. The thunder modulated its sharp blasts in two notes. The lightning, subtle, a bit rhetorical, preceded the thunder like a prediction. They had run hand in hand to Nina's car. And perhaps it had been that, the magic moment that had made the following moment possible: there is a sense of holiday in running to take shelter.

She tossed the keys to him and sat in the passenger's seat.

"You drive," she said.

"Where should I take you?" he said.

"Wherever you want."

He departed after a moment of hidden faltering, the masked terror of making a mistake. Directly to my house might seem brutal; back to her office seems as if I want to dump her off; if she wanted to go to her house she would have given me the address. Cigarette, key, check the mirrors; ignition, first gear.

There is always something to start up. Motors to warm.

Directions, forks in the road, deviated routes.

She wasn't speaking.

He left the city with the rain lending music to the silence in a cloud of woodwinds, the windshield wipers beating the time.

Inside of herself, Nina was repeating an oath, a calming prayer, like a secular mantra, for the use of that divine part of herself to which she never, or almost never, had access: "Suspend judgment, suspend judgment, suspend judgment."

She still possessed the vice of weighing the worth of men. She had been that way in her youth, imagine how much more so now, walled up as she was by her forty-four years in a prison of disdain: you prefer the young girls, you poor slob; you are just like the others, unfledged, a fragile ego, a craver of fresh meat. But Paolo no, Paolo maybe, Paolo in any case . . . She looked at him out of the corner of her eye: a nice, strong profile, he drove well, commandingly, notwithstanding the downpour. The last houses on the outskirts of town had already been left behind, and the car sped along, a wall of water in front of it and two of weeping trees on either side, poplars, dripping beeches, their trunks shiny, the asphalt sending up a fine spray. She reached over and turned on the car radio, risking appearing weaker, like those women who want violins as background music. Naturally there were no violins; a public official with a pronounced Bari accent was decrying some misdeed on the part of someone. She didn't dare change the station. Paolo was smiling at the road.

"You don't have a tape?" he asked.

"A what?"

"A cassette tape, some music."

Nina rummaged in the glove compartment. She rejected Lucio Battisti, who would have been too obvious. She handed him Duke Ellington.

Paolo got onto the highway.

Nina would have liked to ask him where he intended to go. She had a meeting at four, had to write a summons, was expecting some phone calls. She didn't speak. The rain, the trumpet, the music in the compartment of an automobile. It is a poetic world. You can inhabit it, take refuge there, forget.

After Duke Ellington, there was Tom Waits, Billie Holiday, Sonny Rollins. Then Chet Baker, Laurie Anderson, Janis Joplin, Carla Bley and her band, Charlie Parker.

And finally, he, Lucio Battisti.

Paolo got off the highway, singing along with the tape deck: "Yeah, traveling, avoiding the potholes, but not falling into your fears; traveling real easy, without grinding your gears; traveling, slowing down only to speed up again . . ."

Its nose parked against the drenched sand of a dune, its headlights on, the car was still and warm, banally uterine; its windows fogged over, it palpitated from the long stretch of highway it had traveled.

"Where are we?" Nina asked in a faint voice. She would have liked to say, but don't you know what time it is? What kind of bright idea was this? I'm not some kind of artist or something, you know, a film every six years. I'm a woman who works for a living.

"Versilia, I think. Forte dei Marmi?"

"This is called kidnapping," Nina said softly. Paolo turned toward her: the gray light on her small tired face, an afternoon out of time, and how she had been, how she had let herself be taken away from the office, quiet, wrapped in music, like a courageous child who confronts a mother yelling at her, only to play in the courtyard until late.

"Did I get you in trouble?" he asked.

"Yes."

"Are you very angry?"

"No."

He thought about saying something funny: on top of kidnapping, can I add a little sexual abuse? Instead, he remained silent, savoring that monosyllable of hers, as she sat in demure anticipation.

She was a woman, no question about it, and he had been the stupid one, as stupid as the newspapers, to doubt it. Only women can look at you in that way, waiting; they have the grace to let themselves be transported, the taste for losing—weight, surroundings, contours.

"I love you," he said finally.

Nina touched her hair. The hairspray she had put on her

short locks before the hearing had stiffened. I look like a porcupine, a hen, a pincushion.

"Did you hear what I said?" asked Paolo calmly. He felt strong. He would have happily begun driving again.

"Yes, I heard," said Nina.

"And you have no response?"

"It wasn't a question," said Nina. She regretted it immediately, but she had said it. Words were like that, always against her. She used them, they were the tools of her trade. She always won; she knew how to express herself so well. Words obediently played their part in her summations, and her clients always got off with meager damages, absolved, reintegrated back into the world. In her private life it was the opposite. Words played bizarre tricks on her. She said too many of them; irony stuck to her like some kind of malicious glue. Her body blossomed with boils, illnesses, loneliness. With words she condemned herself.

Paolo started up the car again. "I'll take you back to Milan," he said.

It was dark, and the rain had thickened with hail. Paolo drove this time with a different kind of fury, passing other cars, heedless of the downpour of droplets ricocheting off the windshield that reduced visibility like a fog.

The car radio was silent. So was Nina. She was afraid: her car had never done 180 km/hr, she didn't speed like that. Its chassis was of a more utilitarian kind that could not easily handle those speeds. The car was a little, ungovernable body flying over the pavement.

"Paolo . . ." she said, her voice hesitant.

He took his eyes off the road: they were full of tears.

"Paolo, I didn't mean to offend you."

"Don't worry. Everything is fine. I'm the one who is an idiot. I'm never satisfied, always in pursuit of mean, cold women. I'm a masochist. My wife was a shrew, the woman I had before that piloted helicopters. The girlfriend I had in high school was on the honor roll and treated me like an idiot. There is obviously something wrong with me. Ah, but that's it, no more. You will be filed on my computer under 'L.A.'— last attempt."

During his catharsis, in his effort to unburden himself and to wound, Paolo did not see the two lights standing motionless in the middle of the lane.

Nina had been expecting the impact.

She knew that she was going to die from the moment in which, with unexpected grace and ease (two qualities she had never previously possessed), she had tossed him the car keys: you drive.

THE FLIGHT

OF THE ELEPHANT

Claudia Salvatori

My pleasures are empty
but I prefer them to yours,
which are ever full of nothing.
—Iginio Ugo Tarchetti, "History of an Ideal"

Two hours on the train, and then two more in line to get into the club; what a hassle. But it's worth it for an excellent night of dancing.

I came with two guys and a girl. One of them, a guy about thirty-five years old, an "unemployed lover of DJs" like in the Marco Masini song, wears a bandana like Vasco Rossi and calls himself a fascist; he gets all excited about Nietzsche's superman and all that junk. He talks to me the whole time about Ezra Pound as if he were his brother. The girl is totally hot, with long, luxurious black hair and two big mama's tits, but she acts like a man. She smokes in the no smoking area and doesn't give a shit, kicks her army boots against the seats, spits on the floor, and rocks back and forth holding onto the railings. She has a little sparkling button in her left nostril, and I know she has another one (she showed it to me) in her clit: she said that getting pierced down there was like having an orgasm times a thousand. I try to imagine what this cyborg sexuality must be like, with artificial members that extend and enhance your erogenous zones: it sounds like fun. The third is this quiet and aloof bisexual guy, phony sweet, with short blond curls and the air of a sulky boy. He complains that everyone wants to fuck him because he's so cute. He wants to grow old and get ugly so that people will "love me for who I am." I think he works in a boutique, but I'm not sure.

"When you're old and ugly," I say, "no one's going to give a shit about you."

I shouldn't have ragged on him like that, maybe I was too harsh. But I don't really care. I've had enough of these people who constantly blabber about themselves. These three are totally unimportant. They're silly and annoying. They serve my purposes only on Saturday so I won't die of boredom on the train, which goes so slowly in the darkness, without any fucking thing to look at outside but the stream of lights along the tracks that flash by and hypnotize you like an optical illusion.

The name of the club is Amnesia.

Only a few years ago, when I was a little girl, I lived around here: I mean, I was born here. I came into the world the same day that Amnesia opened, in September, Virgo with Gemini in the ascendent. My house was right near the huge billboard for the new dance club, at exit seventeen on the state highway—it was a huge bluish-white flying saucer that seemed to hover in a halo of milky haze in the middle of the road, between the silhouettes of two hills like the ones in *Close Encounters of the Third Kind*.

Many people that night thought they saw a UFO. When I get totally jazzed and I really want to blow people away, I tell them that I was born on the night the Earth was invaded by Martians, under the sign of the virgin alien.

I come into the club. I'm already pumped up in that good way, excited and happy (I crack up when I think that it wasn't the stork that brought me but a spaceship). It feels like the bow of my ship is parting a liquid wall of music, light, aphrodisiac smells, and the radioactivity of scattered longings and desires.

They promise you everything, and everything seems possible.

I'm looking for my ecstasy. The kind I like.

My ecstasy tab is pink, with the shape of an elephant's head stamped into it. It reminds me of Dumbo: flying on ecstasy is strange and funny, the way that little elephant with the big ears was. It's an impossible flight. It makes you want to cry and laugh; it's weird at the beginning, then seems natural and almost real, like when you dream you have wings, and you wish you could live that trip every single day of your life.

This is what the drug does (though it isn't right to call something a drug that makes you feel normal while normally you don't): it lets you feel right. All the people around you are a shitty bunch of assholes. When you first meet them, they seem excellent; then when you get to know them, you're totally bummed out because they are so stupid, egotistical, and empty. Ecstasy lets you see them the way they should be, always marvelous. It modifies all the bullshit they say by making your brain send out some substance that changes your perceptions, improves them. It lets you live the kind of life you don't have, the right kind; it lets you talk to angels.

And having sex on ecstasy is awesome. It's like a 3D porno film of whatever you want, a nebulization of sensations that bathes you, exciting every part of your body. It's not only about a cock and a cunt rubbing and banging together, it's much more. It's like coming out of the shower with tiny, warm droplets covering your skin, your hair, your shoulders, your nipples, clinging around your belly button, to your pubic hair, your lips, your eyelids. Your whole body is an organ of pleasure. You are fucked right down to your soul. You are like an enormous heart that receives boiling lifeblood, and the pumping, the boom boom of percussion instruments bursts open your chest, kicking you in the uterus over and over. Others are outside and inside of you at the same time. All differences fall away, all isolation. You love everyone and everyone loves you. The thousand dancing bodies around you could be just one, and you immerse yourself in them as if in a sea—shouts, leaps, turns, whirls, dances with the cunt (didn't some famous dancer call them that, who was it?). In your dance you unlock all of the energy you have down there, love and pain, rage and longing, betrayed hopes and dreams of happiness. You can do everything with the cunt, destroy and save, kill and heal.

It is clean and healthy, the sex from ecstasy: you don't risk AIDS, nothing happens that you don't want to, people are like images, and you are in the hands of a divine creature who loves you, knows and understands you, and is as able to dry your tears as he is to make you come by licking your clit.

And in the exaltation of all this movement at 120 decibels, in the insane vortex of colors, of arms and legs seemingly detached from bodies being shot out of amplifiers, all is motionless. Or at least I perceive it as at rest, calm and pure, like one of those funerary sculptures of dead little boys on which women bestow kisses, a good *Dylan Dog* story; a world that is dead and at peace, full of defunct myths (Jim Morrison will never again be able to delude you, where he is now), and of beautiful, young corpses on top of me, under me, like the marble of a tomb.

He suddenly appears before me: he is beautiful like a solar eclipse. I say eclipse because, in orbit around the dance floor, he passes in front of the mirrored ball and blocks it out; I can only see his black form outlined in a twilight of thumping music.

Tall, sinuous, long electric-blond hair, he is wearing shiny spandex pants and a white tee shirt with Kurt Cobain's face printed on it. He has a rock star's face, its features animal-like but delicate, sensual, the skin taut and unreal looking, covered with white pancake makeup. He is a fabulous erotic clown, possesses beauty surpassing the beauty that I fantasize and project outside of myself.

We look at each other, and a spark of interest passes between us. We begin to dance for each other, each of us displaying himself in movement so as to attract the other. Our sides lightly brush, our long hair flying. As we approach each other, our dance becomes more personal and intimate, more engaged.

We smile at each other.

"Hi!" I shout, my voice unable to rise above the volume of the music.

"Hi!"

"What's your name?"

We shout our names (I can't understand his) and our ages at each other: he is twenty-two, I'm eighteen.

"I'm an alien! I came down to earth in a spaceship," I joke.

"What?"

He doesn't understand, but it doesn't matter.

From his appearance, my shadowy blond boy is everything I've been looking for: he is perfect, as long as he doesn't talk. I imagine his tenderness and his courage, his sense of humor and his generosity, and I know that he will be different from the usual guys who take you for a fool, and that he will love me forever, "you at least in the universe," like in the Mia Martini song. As long as he doesn't ruin everything by opening his mouth and beginning to talk bullshit. You could love the whole world, if it would only stay silent.

The boy makes a gesture with his hand, waving me over to the bar. I follow him, and we still haven't touched each other physically, even if in our heads we are already more than close. We've sniffed, licked, clung to each other, and screwed to the point of exhaustion. Providing that he doesn't start talking and telling me who he is and what he does. And yet, god damn, he starts telling me that he is an initiate of I don't know what church of Satan, obviously to make himself seem more interesting. "Nothing to do, you understand, with those maniacs that dig up cemeteries and pour blood on themselves. Ours is a responsible choice of beliefs."

Another satanist, the usual head case. Why do people always try to make themselves so interesting? He's a boring jerk like the others. For a little while, I enjoyed thinking that he was a mix between Arthur Rimbaud, the blue prince, and the vampire Lestat. But why can't you ever find someone who is not a put-on, someone who is special, really special?

I'm no longer listening to him. I'm looking at the dead face of Kurt Cobain. (I don't find his suicide at all incomprehensible; I think it's excellent that he told everyone to go to hell when he had albums in the Top 10 and was up to his ass in success.) I look at the living face of this guy what's-his-name, with his lips moving, and I'm thinking, "Be quiet, be quiet, be quiet."

I drag him into the club's sumptuous bathroom, full of pink velvet and hot babes that eat him alive with their eyes. They stare at me burning with envy. There's a short guy with a dark, badly trimmed beard and little round glasses who is talking on a cell phone.

We go into the last stall and close the door.

He stretches his arms out in an ironic gesture of surrender, as if he were giving in to me. I lower his tights, revealing a penis that is pinkish like a rosebud, very graceful, with a little glans suffocated in folds of flesh. I play with this sleepy organ a little while. I tickle it, tantalize it, grasp it, caress it. It doesn't get erect, and I'm not able to slip my favorite condom on it— ultrathin violet-colored with ribbing—if it's not hard. I could try to take it in my mouth, but then all of those horrible images from anti-AIDS commercials come to mind, with all those infected people giving off a green glow like the Hulk. How can I be sure that he didn't get the virus from some woman who got it from her husband who got it from a hooker who got it from her client who got it from a bisexual guy who got it from some woman who got it from a drug addict?

Then I say, what the fuck, you'll never do anything if you're always thinking about AIDS, and I begin to lick his balls. I

tease him with my tongue, I suck him between my lips, I taste
the flavor of his sweet albumen: still nothing. Soft and sali-
vated, it slips right out of me.

Maybe it's because of the alcohol and the pills.

Now he stops me, respectfully, and he assumes control of
the game.

He makes me sit down on the toilet and spread my legs.
He takes the zipper on my skirt and unzips it from the hem
to the waistline (a thing that always excites me—it makes me
feel like someone is opening my body all the way from the
bottom to the top). Then he lowers my panties, rolling them
over my thigh-high stockings down to my ankles, and bares
my breast. I sit like that, like a doll, less than dressed, more
than naked. He begins to softly run his member along my
neck, through my hair, in a gentle, patient caress. Then it descends to my chest, where I hold it for moment, squeezing it
between my breasts, pressing it against my belly in slow circular motions. His thrusting against me becomes more urgent,
more ardent, but he does not yet have an erection.

He trembles slightly, tenses, breathes heavily; so concentrated, closed within himself and within his unappeasable desire, he is like a dead person, or someone about to faint. He
is trying to satisfy himself mentally. Perhaps he is using the
friction between his absent erection and my flesh to wear down
to and expose another organ, one buried within the gray matter
of his brain.

I feel sympathy and gratitude for this odd boy who, without
abusing me, delights me by involving me in his imagination.

He kneels between my legs, presses his mouth to my labia
(he too could care less about AIDS), and penetrates my cunt
with his tongue. God, he has something right on the tip of it:
a stud, a tiny, pointed metal thing. He plunges it in, pulls it
out, presses it against my clit, then begins again, over and over.
It's great, it's to die for, this cyborg sex. Outside, the short
guy's cell phone has not quit ringing for a second (it can't be
that so many people are calling him because they care, so he

must be dealing). I associate that annoying *ring-ring-ring* with the orgasm that explodes in my head, with that metal prosthesis rhythmically stroking inside of me. I lose consciousness of everything around me; or rather, I suddenly come before being able to regain consciousness.

He stands up and rests his inert cock against my belly, leaving two fingers inside me and moving them slowly so that my orgasm diminishes gradually, like the sound of an echo or the circular ripples from a stone tossed into water. He murmurs, sighs, is traversed by shivers. Perhaps he comes too, somehow, by reflection, by absorbing my physical sensations and converting them into a curious moral pleasure.

"Shall we go?"

We leave the disco in the dust. I have taken another tab, and he too is "ecstatic." We feel this incredible sense of well-being coming upon us. We hold hands, intertwining our fingers, and remain welded through them.

I don't know what neighborhood I'm in (oh shit, I've forgotten everything, except that I know how to read and write!). I'm walking around in some small piece of hinterland that could be located any place on the planet between America and the third world.

I look around me: over there is a parking structure, over here a gas station with a tanker truck filling up the pumps, straight ahead the Coop with a neon sign (an "o" is burned out, so it reads *Cop*), and behind a Chinese restaurant that is closing. A skinny Chinese man, with his bones sticking out all over from hard work, his face drawn and tired, is dumping a bucket of water and rotten cabbages in a barrel. I raise my eyes and read the electronic board indicating the temperature, 27 degrees centigrade: 27 degrees, this much at least makes sense, you know that it must be hot.

It's insane: I don't know where I am, really.

I'm not afraid or worried. A diabolical hilarity instead sweeps over me, like I used to feel a few years ago with my girlfriends from school when we would just laugh like idiots for no reason at all. I'm having fun, like when I go into sex shops. The fake cocks and cunts put me in a good mood, like the toothless smiles of nursing infants do. You go into these stores containing all the things people want without knowing how to admit it, and you finally see it all laid out in one place, in a shameless, endearing orgy of objects, and you leave thanking heaven you have nothing to hide, feeling better and freer.

We go down into an underground walkway, still holding hands, and we act like idiots a little. I shout and run, dragging him along behind me. I climb onto his back to ride him like a horse, and he lifts me up and spins me around. I laugh like a witch on a bright spring night. It stinks of piss. It seems like half the people in the world have urinated in here. The ivory-colored tiles are streaked with dried yellowish-orange filaments. The odor mixes with the generic smell of the city: preserved foods, carbonic acid, smoke, sewers, gasoline, and I think I like it that way. I don't know how to express this very well, but this piss left here and there wherever it falls is rightful. It's nasty, but nasty in a rightful way, not like the endless sickening bullshit that people always talk, and all their fine feelings. This is my world, I love it, and in all my melancholy I'm at home here.

"My car is nearby. I'll take you home."

I double over from laughing so hard. I don't know where my home is, I tell him in one ear, sticking my tongue inside it.

"So we'll go to my house."

We climb into his car (a long, silvery thing that looks like it could break the sound barrier). We take off, driving fast. I rest my hand on his thigh, the one and only place it should be right now.

He tells me that he has his own apartment, has money, works in his father's store. They install televisions, satellite dishes, etcetera, boring stuff like that. I turn on the radio and lean back against the headrest, rocking my head to the music. I push my hand even deeper between his legs.

We go faster and faster in the heavy, humid night.

The headlights lash the dark ribbon of road. I slip out of my panties and skirt. I work my hand under the fabric of his pants and touch his silky, soft cock.

It must be gorgeous erect, long and large, white like his painted face.

He quivers, but it doesn't get hard. Fine with me.

I realize that I'm dying with desire to feel his impotent cock against my clit and the opening of my vagina (penetration is only one way to come like any other). What I want from him, right now, is his sweet cock to fuck and to swallow, to make my own.

"Stop the car as soon as you can," I whisper to him.

There was a curve, and he didn't see it, distracted perhaps by my fingers: we're flying, almost hanging in midair, like those dancers that give the impression of being able to suspend themselves for an instant at the top of a jump. My heart skips a beat; I have no time to think.

Then down.

A violent impact slams us from one side to the other. The seatbelt snaps me backwards like a slingshot in reverse. The tires are skidding totally without traction. It is a sensation that reaches me directly through the wheels, horrible and riveting. I scream like on a roller coaster at the amusement park. A vertiginous sliding, a collision that prolongs itself in other collisions, a chain of them, the sound of glass shattering, the seatbelt still restraining me.

We come to a stop against something: a wall, a high-tension fence? No, it is a billboard with an ass on it, an enormous ass illuminated by one of our headlights (the other must be broken), suspended above us like a full moon.

We ran off the road, what fun.

I detach the seatbelt and stretch myself carefully. It doesn't seem possible that I'm really unhurt. A little suffocated giggle comes out of me—the fear too turns out to be nothing but a big joke.

Claudia Salvatori

I turn towards the boy. He is lying on his back on the car seat which has collapsed backwards. He moans.

"What's wrong?"

He moves his pupils slowly. His lips form a silent, incomprehensible word. Then a beaming smile, as if he's achieved something, spreads across his face. He was only playing: he doesn't have a scratch on him either.

We are alone in the compartment of the car, in the suburban desert, like the nonexistent astronauts from the phony spaceship that landed on the day I was born.

No one to check up on us, no rules to follow, no normality, just the ecstasy.

I climb on top of him and undress him, grabbing at and yanking the printed face of Kurt Cobain. He has a body that looks like it's made of milk, voluptuous, with tiny nipples that you'd like to bite and make bleed. I kiss his upturned and astonished eyes, the half-open mouth that reminds me of that of a praying saint. As a little girl, not many years ago, the little statues of saints and christs would excite me, their beautiful wax faces seized by agony as if in an erotic passion; their open hands the hands of sleepers, their fingers like sea anemones, their bodies enraptured, pervaded by aching sweetness as they swoon. I've always confused ecstasy with something missing, with losing one's senses. During the long summer afternoons, I used to pretend to faint and would throw myself on the bed. The idea of falling in a faint provoked a kind of agonizing languor in me that made me twist and turn in restless desire on the sheets, already impregnated with my smells. I felt totally erotic, from head to toe, but would deny myself an orgasm. I didn't touch myself because I wanted to remain full of that swooning sexuality, feel it swelling inside of me until I could no longer bear it. I breathed deeply, lying prone and motionless, waiting for the excitement to drain away, not down out of my clitoris, but through my whole being, in a vaporous haze mixed with the accompanying shadows of the room.

I am on top of him, grinding myself against his delicious,

defenseless, and vulnerable body. I rub my erect clit along him, feeling shocks of stimulation shooting through it. I dance lightly upon him, caress him with my sex; I redraw him, tracing out the mental map of my desires. I don't know what I am doing, but I know it is beautiful, perfect, the thing that I need. I am fucking and flying in ecstasy; I am screwing all the gods of rock, dead and ascended to heaven. I love my black angel—I am raping every part of him with my hands and my cunt, leaving sticky loving moisture on his thighs, his belly, his hips. His face shines in tenebrous pallor. I bury my fingers in his blond hair, I cover him like a sea, I catch up his tender penis in the cavity of my sex. It is like taking a child; it makes me feel almost sad. Maybe I will return to the time I was a child, when I was bounced on my grandfather's knee, when I loved Dumbo, when I still felt loved and protected, swaddled in the world's affection. I cover him with kisses and cry, the tenderness I feel is killing me. I feel almost as if I had an oyster between my labia, a soft sea creature that I could devour. I contract the muscles of my vagina, unexpectedly stirring new sensations. I relax, and I bathe him once again.

He is shaken by a brief convulsion. A thin line of blood is drying on his temple (didn't he come out of the accident unscathed?). He must have hit his head against the windshield in the spot where it is cracked in a spiderweb of radiating lines.

I take his head in my hands and lean my face close to his. A little tremor, then a kind of yielding, and he exhales into my mouth. It's not possible that he is really doing this, it must be a joke. He can't be dead—it can't be that I inhaled his death while embracing him . . .

I can't believe it's true. But if I believed it, it would be the highest and most overpowering erotic emotion I've ever felt.

I decide to shrug off believing or not believing. It is what it is.

I then obliterate myself in a powerful orgasm.

It is too much. I scream because I want to keep him with

Claudia Salvatori

me so that it can never end. I come furiously. I feel like my brain catches fire and burns. I die with my boy.

It is the flight of the elephant (from the alien spaceship on which I arrived from outer space), a night that is "different, but truly different," like in the song by Ron.

The perfect night that I've always invoked.

The night of my first and only love.

THE PUNISHMENT

Cinzia Tani

I got my period that day, as always unexpectedly, seeing that I never keep track. I was running with the others down the beach, getting ready to dive into the water, when I felt the usual painful spasm, prelude to a river of blood. I stopped short at the water's edge, infuriated. My friends shot by without even looking at me and leaped into the water splashing and shouting. I have nothing in the cabana, neither pads nor tampons, and so I am forced to go back home. My mother is in town today, and will not be back until lunchtime. In the middle of July, in deadly heat, she finds every excuse to go and check up on my father at the office. It is noon. The boardwalk that runs from the shore up to the beach club is white-hot, and I have to run in order to keep from burning my feet. I put on sandals and shorts and get on my bicycle. The beach house we've rented this year is not far. I'll go ask the au pair if she has something for me. Even at fifteen years old I still have to be chaperoned. The au pair has been here for two months, and not only has to take care of me—the agreement is that she also has to look after the house during our vacation. In the afternoon she is the one who takes me to see my friends, and then she comes back to pick me up for dinner. She is young and very cute, English, and Mom thinks that she can also help my brother and me with the language. Stefano is four years older than I am. He hates the sun, and at this hour he's usually home sleeping because he stays out late at night. There is no one around outside, no sound, and it feels like I'm pedaling in a cloud of heat in the middle of the desert. I've arrived. I open the gate and drop my bike on the lawn, like I always do when my father is not around to yell at me that I'm killing the grass and that he's surely not going to buy me another bike, etcetera, etcetera. I come into the house. Finally a little bit of cool. I go into the kitchen, but Josephine is not there. She was here a short while ago because the water in the sink is still running on the breakfast cups that need to be washed. I turn off the water and eat a banana. I walk through the dining room, through the living room. I hate this insistence on keeping the shades closed to keep out the sun. I don't like it when it's dark in the middle of the day. I am about to call her when I hear low voices coming out of my brother's room. Now I'm in front of the half-closed door. I peek through the opening and see them. They're so stupid to keep the door open! It's an amazing scene, like nothing I've ever seen in the magazines that my brother sometimes forgets in the bathroom. I am horrified, or maybe entranced, I'm not sure. I only know that I am unable to move and that I see everything, from begin-ning to end. Then I go into my room. I hear her leave Stefano's room, go into the kitchen. She realizes that someone has turned off the water, sees the banana peel left on the table, and calls me. When I don't answer she calls again: "Baby!" My name is Barbara, and my nickname is Baby pronounced with a flat "a." She instead calls me Baby with a long "a," the English way, and I can't stand it. She comes into my room, sees me, and her little eyes grow wide, clear blue with surprise and fear. Then, taking note of my indifference, she calms down. She asks me why I'm home; I tell her about my period. She runs concerned into the bathroom to grab her pads. She laughs, teases me, treats me like a little baby. I have this terrible desire to hurt her, to make that happy expression vanish from her face, and I do it as soon as my mother comes home. I simply tell her everything, absolutely everything. The sky comes crashing down. First Mom goes into my brother's room and closes the door, then she shuts herself in the kitchen with Josephine. I hear her shouting, "In front of a child!" Then my brother leaves on his motorcycle and Josephine goes into her room and cries.

Fired! It was the only way it could have ended. I stay home that afternoon, having no desire to go out and see the others. I am afraid I wouldn't be able to resist and would tell them the whole story. I believe that my mother, knowing me, is afraid of the same thing, and she comes into my room acting strangely. She is struggling, I can easily tell, on the one hand with the desire to scold me for spying, and on the other with the wish, perfectly maternal, to protect me from something she feels might harm me. But anyway, I know she is not going to tell me what she actually thinks. Embarrassed, she smiles; she caresses my hair, as if automatically, which I wear extremely long, even if I don't like it at all that way, and she tells me that maybe it would be better if I spent the rest of my vacation at my paternal grandparents' house in the country. She tries to justify her decision by explaining that in July it is difficult to find another girl to come take care of me, that at this point she can't cancel the boat trip she's scheduled with her friends, and that in the country I will surely enjoy myself. I don't say anything. I don't feel like protesting, and neither do I feel like staying here and having to face my brother's guilty expression every morning. So it is decided. We will leave tomorrow.

I pack my bag. I won't say goodbye to anyone, but will leave it to my mother's imagination to make the excuses for my sudden departure. In the room next door, I hear the sound of drawers being opened and closed, coat hangers clicking against each other, the doors of the armoire banging: the au pair is packing, too. She is leaving now, in a little while; there is a bus that stops near the house and that will be here in about an hour. I really hope that she doesn't decide to say goodbye to me. And yet there she is, standing at the door of my room with her red eyes, her hair coming out of her pony tail and partially covering her face. I am expecting a little lecture, or at least some kind of complaint. And instead, she gathers up all the hate she can muster in her glare, and in a low voice, in her pronounced English accent, says: "You are so bad!" Then she leaves. I am hurt. Bad? Why? And what does it mean, bad? I say it to myself all afternoon long, and I finally decide that I like it, I really like being thought of as bad.

The villa is very old, from the sixteen hundreds. We park the car in the big courtyard onto which the secondary entrance opens. A staircase leads up to the door, which itself leads into the kitchen. Around the courtyard are arranged the apartments of the farmers, those who participate more than the others in the family life of the owners. The grand entrance is on the opposite side of the villa and has two staircases leading down from it, one around to the right, the other around to the left and down to the well-tended terraced garden.

Thus begin my days in the country. Completely free, I am entirely unmonitored by parents, young English women, or brothers. My sole duty is to respect the lunch and dinner hours, and to retire to my room after lunch to take a nap. I guess that this must have been a maternal mandate. Even during summer vacation and at fifteen years old, I must spend the first hours of the afternoon in bed with the shades closed and the lights out. But I'm not tired! I protest. It doesn't matter, you at least have to rest your eyes. The truth is that she does not want me out at that hour, when there is no one around to keep an eye on me. She has always feared my exuberance. In any case, in the afternoon I would never sleep. At the seaside

Cinzia Tani

I would put my transistor radio under my pillow and listen to music until it was time to wake up. Sometimes I would leave my room by climbing out the window. It was a dangerous route, two stories to climb down by holding onto things protruding from the outside wall, fragile railings, and branches not exactly robust. I would get down to the garden and, satisfied by my courageous exploit, climb back up again. In the country I discovered instead another kind of enjoyment.

Shortly thereafter, I began to understand that the scene I had witnessed had had a strange effect on me. By day I try not to think about it, but at night, before falling asleep, I go over it all again in the most minute detail. The au pair leaning against the window, with her hands on the glass, her skirt pulled up, her panties pulled down to her ankles, her face turned toward the door, but with her eyes so glassy, so lost in who knows what paradise of the senses, that she clearly is unable to see anything. And he behind, his hands around her waist, his pants lowered, his gaze fixed on that pink "thing," in actuality a livid red. Sometimes the scene appears to me in pieces, like a puzzle: his expression, the lock falling over his eyes, her open mouth, the limp panties swinging between her ankles, the blouse with the parrots that Josephine bought with me in the open-air market in the town. Sometimes the memory scares me, gets the upper hand on my ability to control my thoughts, and then in place of the au pair I see myself. I shiver from fear and immediately try to distract my mind. But in the afternoon, in bed, I feel freer, and I can transform the scene at will. Yes, I am still in the place of the young lady, but the other is not my brother. He is a man I don't know who is trying to rape me. I began to touch myself thinking about these things, and my afternoon nap became an appointment with pleasure, which I would come away from feeling confused, sweaty, and unsettled.

At four o'clock I go down to the garden where all of the farmers' kids gather to play with me. There are two brothers, Piero and Paolo, who live in the biggest apartment of those that you enter through the courtyard. Piero is my age, and in the afternoon, when I am in my bedroom, he waits for me to toss comic books down to him from my window. Paolo is younger, and like his brother never wears shoes. His little legs are always encrusted with mud and dirt. When she can, his mother grabs him and dunks him into the trough that the cows drink at so that she can scrub his legs with an old brush until they become clean and rosy again. At my call, the two boys drop everything and run to the courtyard, but their parents stop them immediately and make them also take their two little girl cousins with them. Piero and Paolo reluctantly obey, since they can't stand the two little girls. But I like Giulia. So skinny, with hair so fine it seems sparse, two big brown eyes out of all proportion to her tiny face. She seems like a Japanese cartoon. She never speaks. "Hi" when she arrives and "bye" when she goes, but she is sharp and intelligent and easily follows the complicated instructions to the games that I make up every day. Marcella is the opposite. Plump, with blond hair always in curls, blue eyes and a little sky-blue dress like a doll's. She is whiny and breaks into tears at every little thing. It is for this very reason that I always feel like picking on her, pinching her when the others aren't looking, locking her in the dark garage or the stables, running away so quickly with the others that she can't find us. Then there is Giovanni, who has a shaved head—none of us ever asks him why. His home is farther away, on the other side of the river, and he never misses an opportunity to play with us. He is always happy, and laughs with his toothless smile. There is another girl who is my age, Rita, who has two older brothers who always bring some friend or cousin with them when they come. And then him. He is one year older than I am, shy and touchy. He is the son of the woman who comes to clean the house and help in the kitchen. She was the one who asked us to call him to play with us, to get him involved in some way so that he wouldn't spend his afternoons sitting on the windowsill in his room whittling with his pocketknife. I like him right away,

Cinzia Tani

from the very first minute. I've always had a weakness for people who are different or who seem to be hiding some secret or problem. When he showed up with his sulky attitude, his absent and unhappy gaze, and his mussy hair, and held his clammy hand out to me, I felt butterflies in my stomach. I immediately made him my favorite partner, giving him attention in whatever ways I could, and receiving in return his bashful but undeniable affection. And yet I sometimes watch him from a distance when he is with Piero or Diego, Rita's brother, and I discover another person. His bleak expression grows placid, his speech more fluent, and the occasional smile will cross his face. Maybe I am the one who intimidates him, or girls in general. In any case, I liked him so much that I began to make him the protagonist of my afternoon fantasies. I imagine that I am playing hide and seek with the group. He surprises me in the root cellar or in the garage, and he blocks my exit. He ties my wrists to the tractor with a rope. He covers my mouth with one hand and with the other opens my shorts, pulling aside the edge of my panties and touching me delicately. When he feels how wet I am, he takes his hand away from my mouth, knowing I won't call out. The variations of this daydream are infinite, as are its locations: the stables, his room, mine, the granary, the attic. I leave my room still excited. I can't wait to see him again. It seems impossible to me that his gaze can continue to be so evasive, that he can still act so coldly fraternal toward me. I do everything I can to seduce him. I choose him for games played in pairs. I go to his house to call him when he is late. I give him little gifts of all kinds. I ask for his advice, demonstrating my respect for him in front of the others. The others naturally notice this, but my choice seems like such a natural one that they share it. After days and days of manifest indifference, notwithstanding all of my obvious attempts, I begin to hate him. I'm in bed with bad cramps, and I have him sent up to me. He is extremely embarrassed, standing at the door and trying not to look at me. I am lying on the bed in a baby doll dress, my tan legs uncovered, in a provocative pose. I try to make him talk, but I can only get stammers and fearful looks out of him. How annoying! And what a desire I feel to mistreat him. To taunt him, I tell him that I have been in love with someone for some days now. He finally looks at me, his whole body tense, poised to ask me the question. I speak before he does, telling him that I love someone who is older than I am, much older, a gynecologist I met the other night at a dinner party my grandparents held for friends of theirs. There were people of all ages there, even kids my age, who were playing stupid games like dancing around the room in a conga line. Then they put on the slow songs, and he asked me to dance. My grandparents weren't looking, and Franco held me tight around the waist. Before leaving, he gave me a kiss between my shoulder and neck, and he told me that one of these days he will take me to the beach. I told the whole story quickly from beginning to end. It is true, but I realized that I gave it a different meaning. I did not like that man all that much, and all evening I had watched the lighted window on the other side of the terrace where we all would meet every day. I was hoping that Federico would see me in my white, low-cut party dress, so different from my usual outfit of shorts and a tee shirt. He stood silently for a second or two, and then he said: "You know, I have a girlfriend who loves me, too. Her name is Maria." Then he ran away.

Maria . . . I imagine a cute blond doll with red cheeks and blue eyes. A sweet and well-behaved girl who inspired sentiments of love and protectiveness. And what am I? A play friend, someone to have adventures with, a girl who is stimulating but also overbearing, someone capable of crying but also of striking fear. There is a little being inside me that wakes up at the first sign of danger, and danger is determined by suffering. The little being rebels against pain. He feels it coming and begins to kick in the belly, to beat with his fists. Then he concentrates and invents something, makes a plan to raise the barricades. He is the one who expresses himself in those

Cinzia Tani

actions that the others call bad, I have nothing to do with it. Now the enemy is Federico, Federico who prefers Maria, and for this reason will never look at me with love. He will never lie down next to me naked on the bed, will not play with my body. I get up; my stomach ache is conquered by my rage. I join my friends in the courtyard. Without me they are an aimless bunch, totally lacking initiative. Piero is reading comic books on the steps to his house. Paolo is loudly bickering with the younger of his cousins about the rightful ownership of a kitten who is being pulled by its legs between the two claimants. Rita is sitting on the edge of the trough to water the cows while she watches Giovanni and Diego, who are competing to see who can toss more grapes into a jar they've set floating in the water. She is waiting for me, even though I told her that I wouldn't be down today. Nevertheless, she is faithfully waiting. She more than the others possesses a form of adoration for me; she would do anything I asked her. Federico is there too, trying to teach Giulietta to ride a bicycle. I watch him from the top of the stairs. His expression is serious and focused, and he smiles tenderly when the little girl, afraid, starts to wobble. His sure hands grasp the handle bars and steady her. When they see me, they all abandon what they are doing and run over to me. There is immediately a renewed thrill of vitality, a quiver in the air. I organize a contest of physical exercises on the lawn in front of the villa, right in the middle of the flowers my grandfather tends with so much love. From broad jumps to hand stands, we go on to backward somersaults. I am a champion in this. I challenge Federico. The others excitedly gather around us. I dare him to do a somersault in midair without using his hands. He looks at me fearfully; it is dangerous for someone who hasn't practiced it. But the others goad him, shout, gesticulate, and he is forced to try. He makes a short dash and spins in the air. He's almost made it, but falls hard on his back. He doesn't move. There is a moment of suspense, as we hold our breaths. Then Federico opens his eyes and sits up, while his eyes fill with tears. "You were afraid! You were afraid!" I shout. I begin to laugh, to make fun of him. I tell him he's a little girl, and the others, hypnotized, begin to imitate me. They ridicule him, even to the point of kicking him in the sides a few times as he tries to get up. "Let's go," I say, "let's leave him here. Maybe he wants to go cry to his mommy." Yeah, yeah, goes the chorus, let's go. I march off like the pied piper, with all the other kids lined up behind me. I turn only once and catch his humiliated and astonished expression. I feel a tremor of compassion and begin to run. We go into the orchard to pick some pears, which are small, hard, and sweet. We climb the trees and shake the branches, filling up baskets of them. But I'm not having fun, not without him. When the others are not looking, I sneak away and run to the front lawn. Federico is still there, sitting on a rock. He is watching a line of red ants on the trunk of a tree. I approach him, but he doesn't raise his head. I kneel down next to him, bend my face down to his, and kiss him on the mouth. He jumps back suddenly and looks at me frightened, saying no! NO! You're so stupid! I shout at him and run away. I'm the one who's stupid, I'm stupid, I keep repeating, feeling my face in flames and my heart hammering.

I go on like this with my little cruelties for days and days. I want to test his resistance, which seems quite durable, given that he doesn't miss a meeting and suffers every torture of mine like a martyr. I find another means to exact my revenge. Or at least I tell myself that I did it to get revenge, but perhaps that is not exactly right. That gynecologist of whom I spoke to Federico came to pick me up to take me to the beach with some friends of his. That day I was sorry to leave my little group for the entire morning, but then I found the idea of taking trips to the seaside attractive. Yes, because being the youngest in a group of older people has its advantages. I can expect to receive attention and care and at the same time be seductive. I began to play with Franco, for instance, almost immediately, coquettish looks, innuendos, innocent caresses. I like to provoke him, change my bathing suit while having him hold a towel around me so that the others don't see, hold his hand as we go to take a swim, hang onto his shoulders as he swims toward shore. All of this works to lower the barrier of age difference between us, to vanquish his queasiness, to make him die of desire for me. Then I let my guard down, and we went further. Not that I particularly wanted to. I have never liked to conclude things but prefer to leave them open, suspended, and imagine their end rather than experience it. At this point, I know that nothing that one has looked forward to for a long time can, once achieved, match in intensity our imagination of it. We began to linger in the car more than was necessary before saying goodnight. We kissed and touched each other between the legs. Ah, unsatisfied desire, how lovely! The veiled gaze upon the foggy windshield, mouths full of saliva, the hands hot upon each others' bodies. We should have stopped there. Instead, one day he brings me over to his beach house. It is eleven o'clock in the morning, and there is no one there. He leads me by the hand into the bedroom. The curtains are lowered, I can't see anything. He pushes me onto the bed and lies on top of me. A few convulsive motions, an unbearable weight upon my small chest, a little pain inside, and then his voice telling me where the bathroom is. I find myself sitting on the bidet staring with sad fascination at the droplets of blood from my lost virginity. I wouldn't want to admit it, but at this moment I shouldn't be alone. I need strong arms to hold me, an understanding smile, a tender look. I'm still ultimately just a little girl! Instead, he knocks on the door to tell me to hurry up because the cleaning woman is on her way. I didn't want to see him again. I felt betrayed; it should not have gone this way. But two days have passed, and I no longer even think about it. I've returned to my adolescent dreams and to my desire to fall in love. The anger over what has been remains, however, and it is Federico who will pay the price for it.

One afternoon before the others arrive, I go to his house. I stop in front of the door and look up. I know I will find him there sitting on his windowsill. I ask him to come down. I bring him into a little room underneath the villa's outside staircase with an entrance onto the courtyard. There is a manhole cover in the floor in the middle of the room. I ask him what it is hiding. It is the black well, he replies. The sewer. I want to see. He says that we are not allowed, that it is dangerous, and that his parents have always asked him to make sure that it is securely covered. I insist, and he raises the lid. It is a real well, deep, full of dark water. He quickly shuts the cover. I have brought you here, I say to him, so that I can tell you something, a secret. We sit down on the floor, and I confide everything about my adventure to him. While I am telling my story, I see him turn completely red, and he covers his eyes with his hands as if to block out the images that begin to hover in the room. I go on until he springs to his feet. Stop! stop . . . he wails over and over. His reaction astounds me, his pain is so evident that it frightens me. I take his hand, which is hanging by his side, and I force him to sit down again. I continue with my story, and during it I look down at his pants. I see that they are expanding right there. I see his zipper rising, the fabric stretching. I stick out my hand . . . He leaps to his feet, and this time takes a step toward the door. I also get up, and I catch him by the sleeve of his shirt. Federico, I call out to him, you are the one I want to be with. Please, do it with me, do it now! He pulls his arm away from me, and looks me in the eyes for an instant. Is it disdain that I see in his look? Slut, whore, and then he is gone. Don't leave! I shout, don't leave, or I'll . . . you'll be sorry!

Later, we all decide to play hide and seek. I look for a place to hide with Rita, and something leads me back to the forbidden room. I am here in the half-darkness. Whoever is looking for us won't find us here, I think. This is not a place for games. I whisper to Rita: "Do you know the black well?" She shakes her head. "You're not allowed to open it," she replies, "it's dangerous." No, come on, I go, only to take a look, and I have already pushed the heavy cover partially aside. We both look down, fascinating by the black water, the depth of the well. Suddenly, the little bit of light in the room dims. We instinctively turn toward the small window, which is framing the round face of Piero. He has found us. Run, I say, maybe we can make it to home base before him. Standing in front of me, she leaps for the door, passing the open well, and is already outside. I also make a dash for it, but I must have miscalculated because the next thing I know I am neck-deep in water. Then it is total madness. My cries, the shouts of Rita, me trying and failing to get a hold on the slippery walls of the well and sliding further down, with the vile liquid rising to my mouth. Someone rushes in and sticks a hand down to me. I grasp onto Piero's fingers, and he is able, after a few tries, to pull me out. I've hurt my leg, which is bleeding. They've called my grandmother, and she sticks me, clothes and all, into the bath tub and scrubs me hard with a sponge. Then she puts clean clothes on me, and with my grandfather takes me to the nearest hospital to get me a tetanus shot. After the big fright, then the questions. Why was the cover off? Who did it? Federico, I say without hesitation. He wanted to show me the black well, and he never put the cover back on.

That evening I'm with the others in the courtyard. My grandmother did not keep me from going outside, but for the first time asked me not to wander too far off and not to play wild games. We all begin to play cards, sitting on the gravel. Then some shouting catches our attention. It is coming from Federico's house. We run there. I peek through the half-closed door. His father, who has been told about my accident, is beating him with a belt, and it is he who is shouting, cursing. Not even a cry from Federico. His pants are pulled down, and his rump is red from the blows. He looks up and sees me. I can't bear to see his expression, and I run away. Later on, I go to see Rita. I bring her comics, candy, clothes, all the things that I know she likes. I ask her not to say anything, anyway there's nothing we can do about it now. I know she won't betray me, I can see it in her eyes.

The next day, Federico does not come down. He is seated on his windowsill, and we call him from below. I am sorry to see him like that, but feeling pity for someone always makes me mad. I begin to make fun of him, ask him if he still has a red bottom, if he needs a pillow to sit on, and things like that. I see the tears running down his face, and I feel like I am going insane with love for him. It just makes me more angry. We all jeer and mock him in unison, and at that moment my parents' car pulls into the courtyard. It is the day of my departure. Summer vacation is over. My mother wants to see the cut on my knee, but doesn't seem particularly concerned about my fall into the well. She tries instead to calm my grandparents, who are still frightened and distressed over what has happened.

I am leaving. My bags are already in the car. First, however, I run to the bathroom because I can't stop crying. I am sobbing with my face in a towel for at least a half an hour. It is not some feeling of guilt that makes me cry, but the fact that the game has to come to an end.

Twenty years have passed. The most important facts of my life, as seen from the outside, are a degree, a part-time job, a husband, a child. What have I lost? The little girl that I was, the bounding heart, the sensuality. It's true, my senses died out little by little in the routines of married life, but also before, during numerous relationships with men. Never again in my adulthood have I felt my body tremble. I miss the muggy afternoons and the fresh sheets against my skin, feverish with exasperated desire.

When my grandfather died, my grandmother left the country villa and moved to the city, to a tiny apartment. Sometimes when I go to visit her, I page through her photo albums in search of the Baby of long ago, and I find her, disheveled, red-eyed, barefooted, in rumpled clothes. But that is how my grandparents wanted me to be, I've always understood it, a little savage, spontaneous, excitable, free of all the artificialities that my family had imposed on me. That, too, is how I like to remember myself. I love that little girl. I wish I could see her again somewhere, hear her speak, watch her while she runs, commands, cries, stamps her feet.

Now the villa is for sale because my grandmother can no longer manage to keep it up, and for a year or two now does not even spend the summer there. Several of the fields were sold some time ago, and the farmers have left the apartments. Only the guardians have remained in the big house. Federico and his wife.

This evening my husband and I are at dinner with Federico. When we pulled up in the car, he was waiting for us on the staircase. I was the one who wanted this meeting to occur, mostly out of curiosity. It was a cold curiosity though, devoid of longing, composed solely of the desire to analyze the passage of time. "Twenty years is not that long," I think, looking at his hair, his same dark and reticent expression, his large hands clasping mine. What must he be thinking? What does he remember? I am used to forgetting hard feelings, but not everyone is as able to as I am. That is just how I am; after a short period of time, the memory of hurt fades. There are people who love to wallow in pain, in bitter memories. They gain strength, anger from it. For me, it is just too difficult to have such thoughts. I brush them off out of laziness.

After the greetings, the presentations to his wife and two sons, Federico seems to erase me as a presence, and for the entire evening devotes himself to my husband. They discuss the problems to be resolved before the villa is sold. During dinner, Maria stays in the kitchen. She doesn't want to join us, even though I insist several times. And yet I would like to observe her better, try to see in her the characteristics of the adolescent she was that deprived me of my first love. She is not beautiful and obviously never was. Her hair is black and kinky, her features quite pronounced, her legs thick. Her expression is obtuse, seems detached from people and concentrated solely upon things. She busies herself with the pots, washes and dries the plates, acts as if she has had to prepare dinner for ten. It is only when Federico, thinking that no one is watching, gives her a slight caress on the arm that the old feelings come upon me with staggering force. That hand! How often I dreamed of it upon me. I would have kissed it, licked it; I would have nibbled his fingers, sucked them.

I think all night about him, while I toss and turn in bed in my old room. I wanted to sleep here because tomorrow morning my husband will wake up early and spend part of the day in the nearby town with the villa's new owners. I get out of bed, and wander around the room barefoot. The unfamiliar contact with the cold floor revives other memories, of the afternoons I went to the window and at the agreed upon moment tossed the comic books down to Piero, of the evenings I pressed my nose to the glass and gazed out at the window below, the one on the other side of the courtyard. That very same window that now is completely dark. But there is someone in the courtyard. I hear footsteps on the gravel, and I see the glowing tip of a cigarette. Even now, as back then, Federico paces underneath my window without looking up even once. But those many years ago the distance between us was short; it could have been crossed easily through will, through desire. Now we live on different planets, and there is no communication between them. He is still a farmer, I have become perfectly middle class, confirmed, conventional, stuffed with commonplaces and formalisms. Nothing about me is out of place, not a hair, a gesture, a word. Everything I do is studied and calculated to make the best possible impression. Is it possible that one can change so much? It is a question that I ask myself only now, since now I can finally remember how I was. I can say that in all this time I've remained uncontaminated, since I've never let anything dirty me, avoiding every involvement and, necessarily, every pleasure. Sex for me was a planned activity, like going to the store or picking my son up at school, inviting people over for dinner or eating an ice cream when my diet allowed.

I watch this man pacing below my window, and a little girl's voice whispers in my ear: call him! He is the attic to be explored, the flight to be attempted, the darkness to be brightened. But how many layers have to be penetrated before the strength to move explodes in me. How much superstructure and exertion. It is much easier to put the embroidered slippers back on and go back to bed.

The next day I wake up late. My husband has already left, and I go walking in the fields, looking for the places of my past. I see Federico near the stables and catch up with him. I ask him some questions, which he answers in monosyllables. The old anger seizes me again. I provoke him: do you remember when . . . ? He blushes, but I do not relent. I try to embarrass him. My former desire is all here, perfectly intact. He feeds the rabbits, then goes into the chicken coop to fix the wire fencing. I am right behind him with my questions, with my tricks. Now we are in the stable. He is turning over the hay with a pitchfork. I continue to play with him. I must be unbearable. Then, suddenly, he raises his head, drops the tool, and comes over to me. He has a strange light in his eyes. He simply says, You were the one who wanted it. Then he throws me to the ground, onto the floor covered with damp hay. I try to raise my head, but he pushes it back down with one hand, and with the other tears off my skirt. In very few seconds my stockings and panties are off, and I feel his stomach pressing on mine. Only for an instant, however, because, pushing with his arms against the floor to either side of my head, he raises his chest and plunges his organ deep inside of me. There, I've found again the scent, the scent that I've been seeking for so long. I smell his body so close to mine, I breathe it in from his armpit. It is a strong odor, made up of fluids and wet fields, of sex and mulched earth, of strength and penned animals. It is a smell I would like to drink, that inebriates and dizzies me. I feel pleasure rising from below up to my head. I feel my muscles grow rigid, my skin stretch. I would like to shout, to cry for joy at the first orgasm of my life after years of pretending. Instead, I am quiet, and ingest the pleasure without allowing it to seep out. After angrily striking me once or twice, Federico yanks me over and face down. The straw is pressing against my lips while he takes me from behind, all the while saying: "What do you want? What did you want? This is it, right? Only this? And from me—right?—as well as from all the others . . ." He is breathing heavily as he speaks, the words are like roaring in my ears. I wish I could answer, explain, but my mouth is pressed against the floor and I can't. I could do it now that I am once again on my back. But I am looking at his contorted face, his mouth twisted into an evil grimace. In his eyes there is no tenderness, no flash of affection or even of sympathy. I feel his whole body tense and then relax. He has pulled out in time, and the hot liquid seems to glue us together for a brief moment. Then he is once again standing, and it is all over. I am still lying on the straw and don't have the courage to stand and straighten myself up. I am afraid of looking ridiculous, with my clothes torn and dirty, my legs dripping with semen, and my makeup running down my face. He pulls up his pants and finally looks at me. The fact that he is standing and I am still on the ground makes me feel small, defenseless, humiliated. The silence terrifies me. I say in a barely audible voice: "I was in love with you and you didn't want me, so I took revenge on you. That is all. I'm saying it now because I sense that I won't have another opportunity." He turns his back to me, tucks his shirt into his pants, and meanwhile confesses: "I was in love with you too, from the first moment. I thought of nothing but you. No one existed for me but you." I raise myself to my knees and ask: "But Maria? Maria?" He looks at me wonderingly, then seems to remember and bitterly says: "There was no Maria then. But what you did marked me for years. How could you have been so bad? The humiliation, the pain, the contempt in the glances of your grandparents—I will never forget any of it. And now I know that I will finally forget you."

He left, and all at once I feel the cold and feel my limbs

hurting. After so many years this is my punishment. I know I will never see him again. My husband will come to pick me up in a short while. We will close the villa, which tomorrow will have new owners, and we will go out to dinner some-where, maybe at the seaside.

GIRAGLIA

Valeria Viganò

You were looking at me and laughing. Maybe you were laughing at the world, who knows. I was looking at your body,
which has no need of clothes of any kind. There was no need
to hide, to cover up. No need to see only parts of you revealed
so as to want to touch you. There was nothing to imagine, all
the typical notions of banally elicited desire put out of joint.
Desire arose out of the combination of gleaming teeth, long
feet, short hair, and hard muscles. Hence, navigating along
your coordinates, everywhere. You laughed because we were
walking side by side holding our books. And you knew that
my book would get thrown down on the sand, and that you
would do likewise, calling me with your eyes, with your arms
held out. Our slow passage along the beach, step after step
looking down at our footprints in the sand, raised our heart-
beats. Our breathing grew heavier as we exchanged glances
from time to time, removing our eyes from Giraglia, the island
that stood before us every day, every hour of the day. Watching
it like a lighthouse marking the known limit of our horizon,

we felt the certainty of being exactly there, for a handful of weeks, between the bed in our room and the refreshing showers after making love. There were only a few guests in the hotel, and we never saw them except in the morning, when, with your croissant and tangy marmalade, you sat with your back to the sea. You preferred to look at me. There is no better season than when the eyes of the other repose upon you, ignoring everything else. All the rest exists as the best kind of background. It was nature in the July heat, the warm waves crashing on the rocks beyond the tables on the patio, the sticky resin of the pines all around. The French murmured at the tables between the waiter and the guests served to intensify the intimacy between us. You laughed and closed your eyes, trembling slightly. The guests saw, but could not easily decipher, the flow back and forth. It was other and far away to them. It was easier for them to understand the currents in the bay, the scudding clouds, the birds diving for fish. The high sun blinded their ill will and unpleasant thoughts from morning until night, and for once the low murmuring blocked out all suspicion. And everything ran along tranquilly, while everyone read their vacation books on the chaise lounges.

We did not use them, but chatted while lying on our elbows, looking at each other from out of the corner of our eyes, feeling each other's hot breath. The beach towel piled with things and with our bathing suits shone forth its bright colors against our nakedness. You got dressed only to go buy an ice cream or a salade niçoise made of tuna, crunchy lettuce, and boiled egg. The flavors of our hunger dressed each meal with salt and oil, with full bites and lips joined. Drinking water greedily from the bottle, we let fresh droplets fall upon our dry skin, and you were always ready, if I would only let you, to lick their rivulets from me and return them to my mouth.

Shameful thoughts, words, and actions do not exist. There is the shame, perhaps, of recounting that which we have already abused through too-brusque immediacy or through syrupy rhetoric. And yet, if I were to say that the erotic can only be

Valeria Viganò

truly intimate between two people, I would be taken for mousy or for a kook. Or I would hear myself called even worse if I were to say that it is indissolubly, in its fullest realizations, bound to love. The eroticism of betrayal is the last refuge of poor, wasted loves. That of seduction, exercised without feeling, a meager gratification of vanity.

When we took our walk, we left behind our towels and our spot near the outcropping of rock. Away from the shoreline, the dunes followed one after another, rising and falling among low, thorny bushes. No one was around, but if someone had come upon us it would have been no concern of ours. We wouldn't have stopped, I knew that. We would have offered the spectacle of two people who could not separate from each other, of breasts fused to breasts, of legs wrapped around each other, of hands clasping hips. We had chosen a cove in the shade, underneath a burning but sheltered overhang. We were naked enough to pay no attention to the sand that entered everywhere. Within your blond hair and in my ass, into your golden fur, inside our ears. And licking your ears meant alternately tasting your soft skin and the hard, clear grains that had found their way into them. I licked them out with little thrusts of the tongue, and your ear shined with my saliva. And your whole face shined as I, like a little rodent, licked and nibbled it. You were the fruit to be nipped and fondled, to be sure. And our sun-warmed bodies slid against each other from that first burning afternoon on, wiping away our sweat and distilling more of it from our dilated pores from the intense energy with which we kissed each other. You always knew how to kiss extremely well. I can imagine you with all your other lovers, who came first and who after. But what *I* could do to you, oh yes—a lover's meager consolation, you will all say. Because it wasn't the number of times you came or the way. It was why. It was because you trusted in your passion and in mine. And our giving ourselves so totally to each other was letting instinct take its own way, and led to our tussles and panting disengagements, our climax upon climax.

Giraglia was closer from the ruins of the tower that we climbed after making love. Laughing and tottering, brazenly holding hands, in spite of everyone and all else. I liked it when you held my hand and led me, because you were taller and more decisive, and your green eyes held sway over my life. And lying on your dark legs, with my head against your still wet groin, I could have believed myself to be that ideal woman that you took me for. You delicately caressed my hair, your strong fingers tangled in my sweaty locks ruffled by the wind. You slowly stroked me, and closing my eyes I felt myself to be totally complete, just barely, for a moment. You could have done whatever you wanted to me, hit me and hit me, rolled me over upon the stone and taken me without asking, one hand around my neck and the other in my ass. You passed your soft palm over my ears, again and again in silence, and for me it was as if we shared the same belonging. There was not a cell in me that did not breathe in you. The rough stone scratched my legs, but you were the most comfortable of bosoms. Without ceasing to caress my lips and trace the outlines of my face, with a knowing touch that leaves its memory like an imprint of fingers upon the flesh, you directed your long eyes and thin aquiline nose toward the cove underneath the tower. You wrinkled your brow and put on your dark glasses. I squeezed your arm, and you raised them and smiled at me. I wanted you for this, for so little, for your wide, tan shoulders and your hard pelvis. I rolled over and buried my face between your thighs. There was a spot left on your bathing suit. My tongue lapped at it, soaking you with saliva. Underneath the stretchy fabric I felt you swell, heard the tremors in your voice. I stuck my finger underneath the fabric and pulled it aside. I was exposing you so that the sun would dry you. Then I let it fall back and cover you again.

She woke up to find her pajamas stuck to her sweaty body. She angrily tore them off. What the hell kind of dream was

Valeria Viganò

that? She felt the linen sheets against her naked skin. The partial darkness entered through the slits in the closed blinds. What the hell kind of dream? Breathing heavily, she tossed and turned in her bed and spread her legs, feeling hot. It was an insane heat, one that came from within. She felt as if she were burning up because she was devoid of any thought at that moment. A ball of fire, of fear. She panted, could not breathe. Because things enter in through the window of one's dreams, and one is always so unprepared. How can you prepare yourself for your dreams? Not even this she knew. She passed a hand over her skin as if it were the hand of another. She passed it down her pelvis, thinking that she had no future. She passed it over her soft breast, thinking that she had a beautiful, unused body. She stared blankly at the ceiling, caressing her forehead, her neck. She brushed her fingers across her nose, her cheeks, closed her eyes. The bed was large. Her foot touched a cold wall. Slowly, wandering under the sheet, she drew close to it. She kicked off the covers completely and pressed her body to the white surface. The wall was hard and icy, but as soon as she leaned against it her body warmed it. She searched, therefore, for areas that were free of her imprint, feeling here and there with her open palms. Against her there was a solidity that repelled her forms. She too had flattened herself out, seeking relief. What kind of dreams, unpleasant and evil . . . what can one ever do to resist the attraction of bodies, the love that such attraction makes us attempt? Sleepless minutes passed. She could not even imagine that the next morning there would be light. She curled up now, and carefully caressed her feet, almost as if they were a brain to be fondled. Moments of lucidity and awareness alternated with feelings of being suspended, in limbo. She was truly naked, truly undressed and unprotected. She thought no longer of the dream, or perhaps she did in spurts, because in some part of herself she felt a diffusing sweetness take the place of the rancor toward herself. How had the idea come to her to get off track like that, to dream a happiness? She could not allow herself to let a dream devastate her. She had tears in her eyes as, ever so slowly, as if she were floating, she passed a hand down between her legs, to the only part that had been overlooked. She knew quite well both how to caress and to caress herself. Her hair had fallen over her face while, with a mixture of rage and pity, she moved around and inside of herself. The anger left by the dream guided her fingers, and her legs, distant from each other, firm, tensed. Her breathing, which the dream had quickened, stopped and held for longer and longer periods. She felt a spasmodic desire to cast off images that would otherwise have pursued her for days thereafter, while she was eating breakfast in the morning or sitting in a movie theater at night. Now she felt neither hot nor cold. She felt nothing, no emotion. She thought of nothing, not a meeting, not a project, not an idea passed through her head. Her head no longer existed. The dampness on the tips of her fingers was her only possible existence. She could prolong the anticipation of her liberty, could come and then try again, and again, to the point of exhaustion. She knew herself well, at least this about herself. It was all her own, not to be shared with presences or apparitions, bit players in her life. It was hers, she sneeringly paraded it in the face of the dream and all its actors. No one could steal it from her. She was alone, lying on the rumpled linen sheets, and for a moment she wanted to prolong it all until the next morning. No one could strike at her, hurt her, no one could be furious with her, ignore her. While she continued to caress herself, she had no fantasies, nor did she have need of them, because they were the thing from which she had to distance herself. From images real and dreamlike that flowed ceaselessly through the region beyond her brain, images stolen once from sight and reproduced in an endless cycle, to the point of becoming a mute parallel life, wordless and voiceless.

Her pleasure arrived with great intensity. She emitted a long, hot sigh, and her hand stopped stroking her skin. She

Valeria Viganò

carried her finger to her lips, she tasted it. Its flavor was familiar and good, like the fragrance of fresh bread. Now she knew she would fall back to sleep. Her eyelids closed slowly, her head weighed more heavily on the pillow underneath. The brief sleep that in a few hours would deliver her again to another vigilant day of activity, and that had earlier been shaken and violated, would give her no other dream. Of this she was certain and felt at peace. The same damp hand that had confidently bestowed a pleasure on her savored even by mouth now instinctively rested against her cheek. She gave herself a final caress, alone, and fell asleep.

Ippolita Avalli was born in Milan and lives in Rome. She is the author of poetry, plays, screenplays, stories, and novels, among which are *Non voglio farti male* (Milan: Garzanti, 1991) and *La dea dei baci* (Milan: Baldini & Castoldi, 1997).

Angela Bianchini was born in and lives in Rome. She is the author of several essays and narrative works, among which are *Le labbra tue sincere* (Milan: Frassinelli, 1995) and *Voce donna: Presenza e scrittura femminile nella storia sociale dell'Occidente* (rev. ed.; Milan: Frassinelli, 1996).

Rossana Campo was born in Genoa and lives in Paris and Rome. She has published several novels, among which are *Mai sentita così bene* (Milan: Feltrinelli, 1995) and *L'attore americano* (Milan: Feltrinelli, 1997).

Maria Rosa Cutrufelli was born in Messina and lives in Rome. She has written essays and novels, among which are *Canto al deserto: Storia di Tina, soldato di mafia* (Milan: Longanesi,

1994), *Il denaro in corpo. Uomini e donne: La domanda di sesso commerciale* (Milan: M. Tropea, 1996), and *Il paese dei figli perduti: Una ragazza in viaggio nella terra del tempo del sogno* (Milan: M. Tropea, 1999).

Erminia Dell'Oro was born in Asmara and lives in Milan. She has published *L'abbandono: Una storia eritrea* (Turin: Einaudi, 1992) and *Mamme al vento* (Milan: Baldini & Castoldi, 1996).

Margherita Giacobino lives and works in Turin. A translator, she has published several novels, among which are *Un'americana a Parigi* (under the pseudonym Elinor Rigby; Milan: Baldini & Castoldi, 1993) and *Casalinghe all'inferno* (Milan: Baldini & Castoldi, 1996).

Silvana La Spina, born in Padua, lives in Catania and Milan. She has published several novels, among which are *Quando marte è in capricorno* (Milan: A. Mondadori, 1994) and *Un inganno dei sensi malizioso* (Milan: A. Mondadori, 1995).

Dacia Maraini was born in Florence and lives in Rome. She is the author of plays, screenplays, poetry, essays, and novels, among which are *La lunga vita di Marianna Ucrìa* (Milan: Rizzoli, 1990) and *Dolce per sé* (Milan: Rizzoli, 1997).

Marc de' Pasquali was born in Milan and lives in Milan and Tellaro in Liguria. She writes for various journals and has published the volume of short stories *Biondo spinto* (Milan: La Tartaruga, 1995).

Sandra Petrignani was born in Piacenza and lives in Rome. She has published books of interviews, stories, and novels, among which are *Poche storie. Racconti* (Rome: Theoria, 1993) and *Ultima India* (Milan: Baldini & Castoldi, 1996).

Lidia Ravera was born in Turin and lives in Rome. She has written several screenplays and teleplays and has published several literary works, among which are the novel *Nessuno al suo posto. Romanzo* (2d ed.; Milan: A. Mondadori, 1992) and the volume of short stories *I compiti delle vacanze* (Milan: A. Mondadori, 1997).

Cinzia Tani has published stories and novels, among which are *Sognando California* (Venice: Marsilio Editori, 1987) and *I mesi blu* (Venice: Marsilio Editori, 1991).

Valeria Viganò was born in Milan and lives in Rome. She has published collections of stories and novels, among which are *Il tennis nel bosco* (2d ed.; Rome: Theoria, 1989) and *Prove di vite separate* (Milan: Rizzoli, 1992).